ABOUT ROBYN SMYTHE

Robyn Smythe is a Scottish writer. Born in the Sixties in Fife, he was educated at Madras College secondary school where he wrote his first full length story. More than three decades later, after a varied working life that has involved being a lifeguard and Post Office clerk, he finally found time to write Fallon, his debut novel. He is married with two daughters, and is currently working on a fourth Fallon novel, Secret Agent Man.

ROBYN SMYTHE

FALLON

The Legacy Series:
Part Three – 'The Gathering Storm'

Grosvenor House
Publishing Limited

The right of Robyn Smythe to be identified as the author of this
work has been asserted in accordance with Section 78
of the Copyright, Designs and Patents Act 1988

The book cover is copyright to Robyn Smythe
Cover design by Brian Jones
Cover image copyright to jpa1999

This book is published by
Grosvenor House Publishing Ltd
Link House
140 The Broadway, Tolworth, Surrey, KT6 7HT.
www.grosvenorhousepublishing.co.uk

This book is a work of fiction. Any resemblance to
people or events, past or present, is purely coincidental.

A CIP record for this book
is available from the British Library

ISBN 978-1-80381-895-5
eBook ISBN 978-1-80381-896-2

This book is dedicated to Ian and Frances.
My Auntie and Uncle who raised me.
I owe you more than words can express.

All my love

Rx

Prologue

Jackson Blaine walked through the main door of OSP headquarters and collected his identification card from the security desk as he had done so many times since he had started at the building. The security guard on the desk made him sign in and even, for once, flashed a smile. Blaine, however, was not in a jovial frame of mind as, all the way here, he had gone through in his mind the massive task he had been given by the suits on the top floor of Intelligence House, archive all the files on to computer was their big plan to bring the archaic paper filing system kicking and screaming into the twenty-first century.

When originally given the job as archivist of the Office of Special Projects, he had jumped at the chance. His master's degree in history from Cambridge, he thought, would be an asset. He was wrong, as the blisters on his fingers bore testimony to. He needed to be more typist and less historian. Blaine, as he always did, wore casual clothes. He was not one of these stuffy historians you see on the history channels on the television, who sit there in front of the camera and spout crap hoping to impress the viewing masses with their knowledge of dates and battles whilst wearing outdated suits and neckties, looking into the camera through half-moon spectacles as their name flashed up occasionally under them as they waffled.

No. Blaine considered himself one of the modernists of recent history, interested in the reasoning behind an event rather than just being a stuck up storyteller. He nodded to the guard and then headed towards the entrance to his kingdom, the elevator that took him down into the bowels of the earth. It had been six months since his appointment to the job and he had spent most of this wading through the row upon row of shelves containing dusty boxes of after action reports and files on missions, some of which were still covered under the national security banner and were not allowed to be made public.

The elevator door pinged open, and he climb aboard, turning to the array of buttons next to the door and pressing the last one. The door closed and the box shuddered as it began its decent. When he first used the lift, he used to request to go to the Captain's quarters, as the character on his favourite science fiction show '*Star Trek*' did but this hilarity only lasted a matter of a week or so as he soon grew bored of it.

The elevator jerked as it stopped suddenly at his floor, and the doors opened on to a panoramic view of what he called his kingdom. Lines of shelves containing a potted history of the OSP, from its inception to the present day. The previous night, he had managed to find the actual memos from the Prime Minister who had been in power when the unit was envisaged. Starting right back at the beginning was always a good place for an archivist and historian to start, you would think.

He walked towards and stopped at his desk, which was no more than a folding table with a chair and a reading lamp. High finance down in the archives! A computer linked to the mainframe at the ministry sat waiting for him to log on and begin today's exciting quest, an adventure of knowledge, as Blaine referred to it when queried about what he actually did down in the depths. He lifted up the lid of the computer and pressed the power button. Instantly, a little chime from the machine told him that it was ready. Gone were the days where you had to wait for an eternity for the damn thing to power up.

This machine was sleek, modern, and above all, fast. He logged in adding his username and password, then reached over for the first of many files he intended to transfer in this sitting, and he began to type, occasionally referring back to the file to make sure he was getting his facts correct. He had considered himself lucky to have stumbled upon the writings of one of the legends of the service, Jonathan Fallon, who had taken it upon himself to document the early years of the OSP, thus saving him a great deal of time and allowing him to jump forward.

'It was a time of change. The world was changing, recovering slowly from the carnage and destruction of the First World War, and there was change in the Fallon household too. Peter, once a baby, had grown into a strapping boy. His red hair and freckled face charmed

many a girl at school. But his outgoing and lively nature hide a strict home life. Although he attended mainstream schools, Molly, his mother, also home schooled him in extra-curricular studies. He could speak fluent German by the time he was nine and French by eleven. However, his mother constantly warned him against using these extra talents in public, and to always act 'dumb' if any of the subjects were touched upon in class, leading to many tantrums and arguments with his parents, caused by his frustration and lack of understanding of why these restrictions were put in place. While his mother concentrated on the academic side, his father, Jonathan, focused on his wellbeing, both mental and physical.

On many occasions, both father and son would be seen running together in the forest early in the mornings before school. His father taught him to track animals using all the signs and smells nature provided. Peter was a strong swimmer too, thanks to many long days swimming in the lake on their land. Both Smithers, their 'handyman,' and his dad, taught the young man to shoot various types of weapons, from small pistols and automatics to larger rifles and sub-machine guns. Peter thought nothing of it, because he had grown up in this world, but some of the parents at his school thought this strange and reported the Fallons on several occasions for what they deemed abuse.

Once his legs were long enough to touch the pedals, Baldwin, the chauffeur, began to teach Peter how to drive, eventually ramping it up to evasion and pursuit techniques, such as one-eighty turns, drifting and handbrake turns. By the age of twelve, Peter could defend himself, with a working knowledge of karate, judo, and taekwondo. He honed his body by doing sets of push-ups and sit-ups in an old barn on the property. His father drilling into his psyche that his skills were never to be used in anger, only in defence. This, however, would come back to haunt his parents when they were summoned by the headteacher of his school after Peter was caught fighting.

Upon investigation, it turns out that Peter had acted like a gallant knight of old, coming to the aid of one of his female classmates, Victoria Aymes, after one of the older boys had been bullying her in the playground, eventually knocking her to the ground. Peter stepped in, and after taking a few punches, landed a well-placed punch of his own across the bully's nose, breaking it, and also made the boy's eyes water.

The bully's parents were adamant that their precious little soul would not do the things he was accused of, and they wanted action taken against the Fallons, however, when the school board tried to press for the child's dismissal, they were blocked by some Government official, who turned up on the doorstep, one blustery Autumn day, and informed them that it would be in their interest and that of the school's, not to press ahead with this.

Between the years of 1929 and 1933, the economies of many countries were hit by what would become called 'The Great Depression'. It began in the United States with the Wall Street Crash of 1929 and would take until the mid-1930s before some countries started to recover. The murky world that both Jonathan and Molly had *once immersed themselves, had also changed. Alliances had been forged and then broken. Others had changed due to the political climate.*

A new threat would rise like a phoenix from the ashes of the defeated Germany, and a new word for fear would enter our language – Nazism. In March 1933, Adolf Hitler was appointed the Chancellor of Germany. In 1935, he reintroduced conscription into Germany, announced that the peacetime army would be raised to five hundred thousand men, and also announced the existence of the Luftwaffe, the German Airforce. This was the first steps on the road to something that no-one wanted, another world war, which the first throws of that deadly dice were made on 1st September 1939 when Germany invaded Poland. Two days later, 3rd September, Britain declares war along with her ally, France. And so, it begins....'

1 – Little Peter

Winston Spencer Churchill was elected British prime minister after his predecessor, Neville Chamberlain, resigned on 10th May 1940. One of the first things he did, was summon all heads of the Intelligence and Armed Services to his bunker in Whitehall. A year later, Churchill summoned Forrester to Number 10, Downing Street, for a meeting. For the first time, since joining the Office of Special Projects, Colonel John Forrester got his uniform out of mothballs. Jericho Smithers had rejoined the Office of Special Projects, or OSP, as the rumblings of war could be heard on the horizon. He was now too old to be a field operative, instead, he became Forrester's adjutant and awarded the rank of Captain.

In his new post, Smithers travelled everywhere with commanding officer, scurrying here and there making sure that his superior instructions were carried out to the letter, as well as being a sounding board for Forrester to bounce ideas off of, acting the voice of reason when those same ideas were downright ludicrous and there to offer alternatives when the time required it.

"How do I look, Smithers?" Asked Forrester as he stood in front of a full length mirror. He craned his neck as he moved slowly around, trying to view every angle.

"It's a bit snug, Sir." Came the reply from Smithers who sat on one of the numerous couches that adorned Forrester's inner office.

"Tell me the truth, why don't you." Forrester said, mocking his subordinates uncomfortable reply. He launched a glare in his direction and then burst into laughter. "That's what over a decade sitting behind a desk does to your figure, Smithers. You should try it sometime."

"I'd rather not, Sir. If it's all the same to you."

Forrester walked across to his desk and sat down. He pulled open the top drawer, from inside, he took out his pipe, and a pouch of tobacco, flipped the flap, took a pinch of brown tobacco, and stuffed it into the bulbous end of the pipe. Smithers, in a poor attempt to gain favour, lurched forward with a lit match. Forrester looked up at him, before leaning forward, allowing the match and tobacco to merge. A couple of puffs and he sat back, Smithers extinguishing the match by shaking it wildly, before depositing it in a nearby ashtray. It was Forrester's way to have five or ten minutes of contemplation with the aid of his pipe before doing something momentous.

The meeting with the prime minister being a good example. He would either sit in his chair, as he was doing now, or go across to his office window and look out at the world. A storm was gathering, both figuratively and in actuality. He did not like it in either context. As head of the OSP since its conception during the first conflict, some twenty-two years ago, he had sent many operatives to their deaths. It weighed heavily on his mind. Sometimes, he had trouble sleeping as the ghosts from his past came back to haunt him. Flooding back into his mind like a paranormal tsunami.

Most of the men from the olden days had either retired or moved on, either up the chain of command or left the service all together. Jonathan Fallon had retired to the country with his wife Molly and their young son, Peter. The K-12 designation was currently vacant. Sure, he had had various candidates taking on the role, but they had either failed at basic training or been killed on assignment. The wall of remembrance that greeted visitors as they entered the main hall of Intelligence House was filled with pictures of fallen operatives and it both sickened him to his stomach every time he passed it on his way in to work, but it also served as a reminder of his past indiscretions.

He took one last long inhale and exhaled the smoke out of the side of his mouth. Smithers had noticed recently that Forrester had also started flicking his tongue against the stem of the pipe whilst it was in his mouth causing a clicking sound. Click. Click. Click. Forrester was doing this subconsciously and for Smithers, it was bloody irritating. He was about to mention it when his boss jumped to his feet and almost spat the pipe out of his mouth.

"Right! Let's get this over with!" Forrester announced brushing past Smithers, almost knocking him down, grabbed his cap and was out the door before Smithers knew what had happened. The Humber Snipe Mark Two staff car was waiting downstairs with its engine running. Corporal Stephen Collins stood with the rear passenger door open as Forrester whisked out of the main entrance and into the car like a tornado. There was just time for the NCO (Non Commissioned Officer) to give a stiff salute before closing the door, moving around the vehicle, and getting into the driver's seat. Smithers came stumbling down the stairs, opened the rear door, and climbed in just as the car left, with a screech of tyre rubber. The Humber was painted olive green, and the headlights were capped allowing only a slither of light to escape.

A small flag fluttered above the left wheel arch signifying the rank of the officer being transported. The streets were dark, no streetlights. Collins navigated through them using the small illumination that came from the car's headlamps and his own street knowledge. Forrester had requested him as his driver purely because of his local knowledge as he had been a cabbie before the war and had connections with various greyer organisations that were known to benefit from the current conflict.

The OSP had gained the reputation of using such people for information and equipment if they were not available through normal channels. This methodology found Forrester in constant conflict with his peers and superiors, but his retort was as long as the job gets done, who cares how you do it. He took some boyish pleasure out of winding up his bosses but came down hard on anyone under his command that tried to do likewise.

However, the men under him treated him like a father figure, who would fight in their corner if they were in the right, but be the first to chastise them if they broke the rules, those rules being written down in the OSP handbook, that Forrester had written several years previously, and made it policy for each new recruit to have a copy handed to them at the start of their basic training.

Basic training for an OSP operative had evolved since inception. At the beginning, they came up through the ranks of the various armed services and if they showed promise, Forrester would invite them for a six week 'feeling out' process, usually held up in the Highlands of Scotland, during which both parties could 'feel' the other out. Now, with the outbreak of the War, training was given over to two quite different units – the commandos and the Special Operations Executive or SOE.

The commandos instilled the military discipline required for an OSP operative whilst the SOE brought the skills required to survive in the occupied territories. It was an uneasy alliance, to say the least, particularly with the SOE. Forrester had many a long and heated conversations with the Minister for Economic Warfare, Hugh Dalton, whom Churchill had given command of the SOE with those now famous instructions to 'Set Europe Ablaze.' Its purpose was to conduct espionage, sabotage, and reconnaissance in occupied Europe (and later, also in occupied Southeast Asia) against the Axis powers (namely German, Italy, and Japan), and to aid local resistance movements.

Those who were part of it, or liaised with it, were sometimes referred to as the '*Baker Street Irregulars*', after the location of its London headquarters. It was also known as '*Churchill's Secret Army*' or the '*Ministry of Ungentlemanly Warfare*'. For security purposes, its various branches, and sometimes the organisation as a whole, were concealed behind names such as 'Joint Technical Board' or the 'Inter-Service Research Bureau' or fictious branches of the Air Ministry, Admiralty, or War Office.

Forrester's approach was to work in the shadows, by gaining as much intelligence as possible, and then making a sure proof plan, rather than bulldozing in with all guns blazing. He had learned some very hard lessons during the Great War and promised himself that he would not make the same mistakes again during this one. The meeting with the Prime Minister was short and sweet. Churchill laid out his vision for the SOE and OSP to work together in Europe, giving both commanders carte blanche when it came to recruitment and training. It was then the two men took separate paths, but it would be the SOE that would get the accolades whilst the OSP stayed in the shadows.

Years later, Forrester would be heard to remark that the OSP was always the bridesmaid and never the bride. He also said, when asked by a journalist at a press conference celebrating the release of his memoirs, that the remit of the Office of Special Projects was to operate separate from the other intelligence agencies and nothing was outside their field of interest. Intelligence matters.

Local investigations. Covert ops. Whatever the head of the OSP deemed worthy of their attention, really.

So, this was why, on a cold and windy Monday morning, Forrester was standing by his staff car watching some soldiers being put through their paces by several NCOs, who were bellowing orders and cursing when someone fouled up. A rope was suspended between two trees over a small gorge which was filled with foul smelling water, or at least they hoped it was water. A man would climb on to the rope, lie on his belly, hook one of his feet around the rope and inch his way slowly along it. The sounds of explosions and gunfire was everywhere. Other troops could be seen sliding down a cliff on a rope, they called this *the death slide*,' several men did perish. A Major strode up and stood in front of Forrester. A salute.

"Welcome, Sir. Major Hugh Matheson at your service." Introduced the officer, "if you would follow me, please."

The two men left, walking together, and Forrester allowed his subordinate to point out the various sights authorised or listed on the usual guided tours. He had done so many of these in the past, Forrester could smell the political bullshit from a mile away. Of course, there would be certain areas and training techniques that would be off limits to the rest of the establishment, but Forrester was not part of the regular establishment, and Matheson was about to find this out as Forrester handed him a signed authorisation from the Churchill himself, giving him free access to all areas.

It was the first time, since they had met, that the Colonel had seen his subordinate lost for words. In fact, his words seemed to stumble from his mouth rather than flow, as if he were sliding down his own verbal death slide. Matheson ushered Forrester into a large non-descript looking hut.

Once inside, they were treated to groups of men practicing unarmed combat. Each man stripped of their battle dress down to a white vest, blue shorts and black plimsoles. They were taught various types of combat which up until the inception of the unit, was guided by the famous Queensbury rules of fair play. The *'don't kick the man when he's down'* philosophy.

Twelve months later, Captain F.E Fairbairn would introduce a different manner of fighting in his book *'All-in Fighting'* which categorised combat into six sections, each with five sub sections, Forrester would later adopt a variation of this manual as a basis for OSP training when he eventually moved their training to the rugged harshness of the Scottish Highlands.

They were about to leave when two men approached the mat. One was heavy built and muscular whilst the other, a mere boy, was of slim build but with shocking red hair. The way this person moved felt strangely familiar to Forrester, who held up his hand and asked Matheson to wait. The bigger man rushed the smaller one, who side stepped, using his elbow to connect with the small of the back of his opponent, sending him hurtling to the mat.

The big man got to his feet, and bellowed like an angry bull, then charged with arms outstretched in an attempt to grab the other man around the throat. With one fluid movement, the small man chopped the arms out to the side and spun around, launching the sole of his foot into the man's chest, sending him backwards, and landing on his posterior.

Seizing his chance, the smaller man pounced onto his opponent, pinning him to the ground, with his knees across his shoulders. He raised his fist, and was about to strike downwards, when the NCO in charge, yelled for him to stop. The young man jumped to his feet and immediately reached down, offering his opponent a hand, which he took. Both men stood to attention before turning to head back to the seated group.

"One moment." Forrester called after them. The two men turned and immediately stood to attention once they saw the rank of the owner of the voice. Forrester walked over to the younger man. "What's your name soldier?"

"Fallon, Sir."

"Fallon?" The shock both on Forrester's face, and in his voice, was evident.

"Peter Fallon, Sir. Corporal. Number Four Commando."

"You seem to have a knack for this fighting thing, Corporal."

"Yes, Sir. My father taught me to defend myself from an early age, instilling in me the importance of only using my knowledge in self-defence and not in anger." Forrester nodded in agreement.

"Can I ask the name of your father?"

"Jonathan Fallon. I believe you know him, Sir?" Forrester nodded, and then turned, hastily making his way back to his car, as if the devil himself was in pursuit. Both Smithers and Matheson had to double time it, just to keep up with him. Forrester stopped and turned with his finger thoughtfully up at his mouth. Brakes were put on by his subordinates.

"That man..." He began.

"Fallon?" Suggested Matheson.

"Yes, him. I want him."

"But Sir! He's only just started his basic training!" Protested Matheson.

"Ah. I see your point." Forrester realised, "after basic, I want him rushed through phase two and then transferred to my office." The phase two of training he was referring to, was when prospective recruits were transferred to the special operations executive for their covert training, whilst the rest of the unit would continue their usual commando training. Matheson was about to protest even more, but was silenced by the Humber door slamming, and the car speeding off.

2 – Sparrowhawk

March 1942, America had entered the war only four months earlier due to the unprovoked attack by the Japanese on their naval base in Pearl Harbour (7th **December 1941**). President Roosevelt would be heard saying that this date will live in infamy.

In occupied France, five miles south of Abbeville, a commune in the Somme department and in Haut-de-France region of Northern France, a man was running through a forest for his life, pursued by grey uniformed German soldiers, armed to the teeth. Jean Mansur was the man running. A member of the local resistance or Maquis. He was a schoolteacher before the war but now used his academic skills in a very different classroom – the classroom of war. When France surrendered on 22nd **June 1940**, Mansur managed to escape across the Channel to Britain. Whilst there, he trained with the special operations executive and became a spy. After training, he was dropped by parachute back into his homeland, and quickly became one of the local Maquis leaders.

Constantly on the move and hunted by the dreaded Gestapo, German secret police, Mansur had managed to stay one step ahead until a clandestine visit to a local chateau, one cold November night, made him break cover and contact London.

He crashed through the forest, caring little to mask his movements. Low lying branches hit him in the body and face. He wiped away the blood from a gouge on his cheek, but this did little to decrease his pace, in fact, it quickened it. Breathing hard, with sweat pouring down his face, stinging his eyes, he failed to notice the sudden drop, and he tumbled down a small hill, landing in a heap in a stream. He got to his feet, looking around like a prey animal that was being chased by a predator, searching for an exit and a way to escape.

The sound of voices, and a searchlight piercing the gloom, made him freeze, like a rabbit caught in a car's headlights. The voices, German, were shouting at each other. A new sound joined the throng. Barking. The maniacs had brought up dogs. He opened his jacket and pulled out his only defence – a Webley pistol with six rounds. Six rounds. Six chances to get away if he used them sparingly.

He was moving again. Across the stream and into more forest. His mood had changed. The addition of the dogs had made his escape more difficult. His original plan was to escape to the coast, '*acquire*' a boat of some sort, and get back to the safety of Britain, but that door was now firmly closed. He needed to contact Britain by radio, and then lead his pursuers on a proverbial wild goose chase. This was where his local knowledge would give him an edge. He knew there was a farmhouse close by, where a local contact called Michelle, would have a concealed radio set.

The only problem was that that was two miles away, and the Germans were between him and the farmhouse. To make things even worse, it had started to rain and hard. Mansur cursed his luck, as he struggled to gain a footing, as the once hard ground, became slippery under foot. At least the Germans would be suffering too, and to him, that was a comfort, no matter how small.

It took him over two hours to travel to the farmhouse. Stopping every so often, to both get his bearings, and listen for any movement from his pursuers. He nearly walked straight into a patrol, as he crossed one of the numerous farm tracks that littered the area, like veins in some huge invisible body. The two soldiers sat on their motorcycle, one on the main machine and the other in the sidecar holding on to the butt of a Mauser MG-34 submachine gun, which was fixed to the outer shell of the sidecar. They cursed the weather too and were trying their best to shelter under the canopy of a couple of trees.

At one point, Mansur crouched behind a bush and levelled his Webley at the one on the motorcycle. His finger curled around the trigger. Luckily, for the Germans and the Frenchman, cooler heads prevailed, and he holstered the weapon, making a detour behind them rather than wasting a couple of precious rounds. He did chastise himself for some time afterwards, giving up the opportunity of transport, but the noise of the gunshots would have summoned more of the enemy, and he did not want to kick the hornet's nest any more than he already had.

A light from the farmhouse window cut into the darkness, like a welcoming beacon of safety, but as he emerged from the forest, he paused. Yes, the light was friendly, but was the person who had lit it? He pulled out the Webley and moved cautiously forward, using what vegetation there was as cover. He made it to the farmhouse wall without raising the alarm. Wiping a mixture of rainwater and sweat from his eyes, he made his way to the side of the window and quickly peered in, before retreating back to the side of the building.

His reconnaissance proved fruitful. There was, as far as he could see, only one occupant – a woman. Slowly, Mansur made his way to the front door and tentatively tried the latch. It was unlocked. He pushed the door open. It creaked. His heart missed a beat and the noise put him on high alert. He waited for the coming storm. Nothing. Strange. He entered the farmhouse. It was warm and inviting but his nerves were still on edge. Looking around as he moved, Mansur noticed that there was a sawn off shotgun on the table, it was cocked open waiting, like a baby bird with its mouth open waiting to be fed.

He moved into the light and the woman turned to face him. She looked startled and glanced towards the shotgun. Mansur, realising he had the Webley out, raised his hands in submission and put the weapon away.

"The Winter is cold…." He spoke.

"…But warmer when there is a fire to warm yourself." Replied the woman.

"Jean."

"Michelle."

They smiled and shook.

"I must contact London, immediately."

"The radio is in the barn. Come." Said Michelle grabbing a jacket from the back of the door. The two of them crossed the opening between the house and the barn, a matter of about ten feet, but still managed to get soaked to the skin. The barn door creaked louder than the farmhouse one as they ducked inside. Michelle grabbed a lantern, opened it, and lit it. The glow illuminated an empty barn. No livestock. Just a broken down tractor and some other machinery. She went across to a stack of hay bales and lifted the top one aside revealing the top of a set of stairs. Mansur helped her remove the others before descending down into the basement. He pulled on a string in the roof and a light bulb went on. She blew out the lantern.

"Come." She motioned to a box sitting in the corner with a cable running from the back up to the roof. She flicked the two latches on the front and lifted it revealing a radio set. Mansur moved quickly, pulling out the transmitter button and a set of basic headphones. He turned a dial on the front, and the set burst into life with a squeal. He started to tap his message in morse code. First, his call sign and then he waited for a response, which duly came. He started to transmit his message. Mansur was about two minutes in, when he and Michelle both froze, as the sound of two car engines could be heard coming from outside, as well as the sound of German voices. Mansur did his best to hurry up his transmission as Michelle went out to look. She hurried back.

"The Germans." They hurried to pack up the equipment and went back upstairs into the barn. Covering the entrance to the basement before going to the doors and peering out via a crack between the panels. They saw two vehicles – a staff car or Kubelwagen and an Opel truck carrying about half a dozen troops in the back. The troops piled out as the truck came to a halt in front of the farmhouse and a Sergeant started barking orders, pointing to both the house and the outbuildings, including the barn.

"Do you have any weapons in here?" Whispered Mansur looking around. Michelle disappeared from sight, reappearing moments later with a pitchfork and a smile. Mansur shook his head in disbelief. He took out his Webley, pulled the barrel down exposing the cylinder, housing six bullets. Six against about ten. He shrugged his shoulders. Not great odds but might be workable as long as they do not have machine guns or grenades. The bolt action Mauser rifle might give them a chance if they could catch the enemy by surprise.

The soldiers spread out. Three entering the farmhouse, but not before tossing a couple of stick grenades in first. The bang of the explosion caught Mansur off guard, and he jumped with fright making Michelle stifle a snigger with the back of her hand. Mansur glared over at her. There was the familiar chatter of machine gun fire and flashes of light as the soldiers methodically cleared each room on the bottom floor before repeating the procedure for the upper one. Silence followed only broken by a shout from one of the soldiers from within the farmhouse. Seconds later, the soldier emerged waving the shotgun in the air. The Sergeant barked again like some rabid guard dog and pointed to the barn.

Again, they spread out, but some took the precaution of using the ruins of a small wall as cover whilst others edged towards the wooden structure. Mansur took up position in one of the empty animal stalls, whilst Michelle hid next to the door, causing Mansur to wave at her and point to one of the vacant stalls off to her left. Stupidly, she waved back and smiled, again. The doors creaked open, and Mansur braced himself, for a grenade being tossed like they had done with the farmhouse, but instead, the soldiers entered one at a time with their weapons raised. Michelle let out a banshee like scream, as she rushed at the first soldier, burying both prongs of the pitchfork deep into his back.

Mansur fired at the next catching him square in the chest. Both fell like dominoes making the way clear for the next one, who fired into the barn. The MP-40 Schmeisser machine gun chattered, spraying the inside of the building with lead. Two more soldiers joined in, firing into the building. The storm of lead left little room for life.

Before entering, the lead soldier pulled the pin from the base of the stick grenade and tossed it to his left, before taking cover behind the wall. BANG! They waited a moment before entering. Both Michelle and Mansur lay dead. The man's body riddled with bullets and Michelle succumbed to the blast from the grenade. The officer, an Oberleutnant (a Lieutenant), resplendent in his black SS uniform, with the lightning flashes on his collar and skull badge on his hat, now that the coast was clear, climbed out of the staff car and with his Luger pistol drawn, strode purposefully into the barn. Rudolph Heimer, the Sergeant, an older battle hardened man, shook his head in disbelief.

"Looks like Oberleutnant Frenz is pushing to get his Iron Cross early." The two soldiers next to him laughed. The Sergeant walked lazily into the barn to see what the arrival was doing. The officer was standing looking at the corpses, first, with a look of shock on his face, it was obviously the young pup's first body and then, as if a switch had been flicked, he pointed his weapon, first at Michelle and then at Jean and fired three rounds into each.

Heimer stood there, his mouth open in shock at what he had just witnessed, making him wonder what tale of glory this uniformed psychopath would be telling with his offspring or his drinking buddies in the beer halls after the war. The young officer nodded with satisfaction of a job well done, turned smartly and brushed passed the Sergeant, coming back out into the yard.

"Well done men. They are dead. Two less dogs to worry about." He congratulated them as he strode back to his car and got in the back.

"Jesus! This is what we have to work with." Cursed Heimer as he ushered his men back into the truck before returning to the barn, tossing two more grenades in, and walking back. As they left, the barn exploded into a ball of fire, incinerating the two corpses, and the evidence, all with one efficient method.

3 – Little Brother

15th **May 1942**. In London, Forrester was summoned to the office of the Minister of Economic Warfare, Hugh Dalton. When he got there, he was expecting another argument with the minister about the effectiveness of the OSP during the current conflict, but instead, he was met at the steps of the building by a Naval Commander, by the name of Fleming, who saluted, handed him a manila envelope, before turning around, and going back inside, leaving Forrester standing there by himself, looking down at the gift. He cursed under his breath, before returning to his staff car, and ordering his driver to take him back to headquarters.

As the car pulled up, an NCO came out and opened his door. He thanked him with a salute, then headed inside, passed the stacks of sandbags, and the two fully armed sentries, who bent their arms across their chest, hand palm down in salute, before snapping the arms back to their sides. He brushed passed Smithers, who was in his usual position, as the bastion of last resort on the desk outside Forrester's large oak door, which led into the inner sanctum, his office.

Smithers knew that walk, and paused before getting to his feet, counting slowly to ten in his head, and then pointing to the oak door. As if following his subordinates cue, Forrester bellowed his name. Smithers knocked and then entered. He found his superior sitting, as he had done many times before, in front of his large desk with two empty chairs facing him. Without looking up, Forrester pointed to one of those chairs.

"Do you know what this is, Smithers?" Asked Forrester looking down at what looked like a classified report on top of a manila envelope, the same one handed to him by the Fleming.

"No Sir. I'm afraid I don't."

"Trouble." He tossed it over to Smithers who picked it up, and read it as Forrester continued, "I was handed this by some snotty nosed naval commander outside the Minister's offices just twenty minutes ago, without a by your leave. It took the bloody man to salute me!" Forrester's face was getting redder by the minute. He looked like he was about to blow a blood vessel. "Have you read it yet?"

"Barely."

"SOE headquarters received that garbled message late last night, from one of their operatives, codenamed Sparrowhawk. It mentions something about a place called La Maison Blanche."

"The White House."

"Yes…yes. I know what it means, Smithers!" Forrester snapped.

"Sorry, Sir."

"Err...quite." Replied Forrester awkwardly, "anyhow, the transmission was terminated before he could complete his message. According to SOE, Sparrowhawk was a deep cover agent, and if he found it necessary to break the silence, about this Maison Blanche, then it must be important."

"I agree Sir, but can I ask a question?"

"Go ahead." Forrester got to his feet and walked to his office window, took his pipe out of his jacket pocket, a pouch from the other one, stuffed some tobacco into the pipe, returned the pouch to the pocket, and then padded himself down as he looked for something to light the pipe. There was a rasping sound and Smithers appeared at his side with a lit match. Forrester stooped slightly allowing pipe and match to connect before standing back up. Smithers extinguished the match, tossing it into the ashtray on the desk.

"Why us?" Asked Smithers, "surely the SOE should be handling this. Sparrowhawk was their agent?"

Forrester took a couple of drags from his pipe before replying. "Yes, you would think so, but those pencil pushers in Whitehall have bigger plans for them and have asked the SOE's little brother to deal with it!"

"Little brother?" Repeated Smithers.

"Yes. One of the minister's underlings called us that, as I passed him after the PMs briefing."

"Stuck up arse!" Cursed Smithers and then, immediately standing to attention, like a schoolboy about to be reprimanded by the headmaster for some indiscretion. "Sorry Sir."

"For what? Being a mind reader. Sit yourself down, man." Said Forrester, the storm of his mood had obviously started to pass. He turned to a now seated Smithers, who was studying the file. "So, what do we do now? Rush head long into God knows what, and get someone killed, or tread cautiously?"

He paused, waiting for Smithers' input, but gaining just silence, as his subordinate was engrossed in what he was reading. Forrester waited another few precious seconds before coughing.

"What? Eh? Oh, sorry, Sir."

"Do you have any suggestions on how to proceed?" Asked Forrester retaking his seat behind his desk.

"Well, we don't know very much about this Maison Blanche. May I suggest we get one of the flyboys to make a pass over it, and get us some pictures so that we can study them and make a more informed plan?"

"Agreed. I'll let you arrange that in the morning then?"

"Very well, Sir." Smithers left, leaving Forrester surveying the report for the second time. Each time he read it, his mind wondered, what was so dammed important about his non-descript chateau in the middle of the French countryside, which would make a seasoned agent like Sparrowhawk risk his life to draw attention to it. He finished by checking the bottom of the report, which stated that the Germans had killed both Sparrowhawk and a local contact. This left a sour taste in his mouth. He did not know either of them, but he hated the useless waste of life in wartime. "Brave people. Brave people." He repeated.

4 – La Maison Blanche

It was almost six in the morning, when the small travel alarm clock rang out its warning for him to get up. A hand appeared from below the covers, searching for the damn thing. After several failed attempts, mission accomplished, and a hand came down hard on the timepiece, sending it careering to the floor, where it bounced once, and scuttled under the cot. A man's voice from beneath the covers cursed, and then they were thrown back, revealing a young man in his twenties.

This was Flight Sergeant Finch Geary, who swung his legs over the side of his cot and got to his feet. He picked up the cheap market bought watch and stared at the time. He cursed. He was going to be late! Geary was six foot tall, with tanned skin. His light brown hair was cut short at the sides and back but left scraggily on top. He liked it that way. It made him look like one of those matinee idols of the silver screen that constantly woo the ladies. His looks, along with his pearly white teeth, made him a magnet for the ladies when he ventured into the local public house when off duty.

Half an hour later, his jeep pulled up in front of his aircraft, the Supermarine Spitfire PR Mark IX, a photo reconnaissance version of the aircraft. The guns had been removed to reduce weight, and the ports were sealed over. As many of the joints and gaps in the fuselage, as possible, had been closed over to improve speed. The cockpit replaced by a sliding hood with teardrop shaped blisters on the side, to improve visibility. Finally, two F.24 5in cameras had been placed in the wings, in place of the guns, pointing down. It could also carry 114 gallons of fuel in its 'D' shaped wings giving it an overall range of 2000 miles.

'You don't fly a Spitfire, you strap it on and fly. It is the most beautiful aircraft I've flown in my life.'

P/O Bob Doe

No 234 & 238 Sqdn

Unlike its combat brothers and sisters, who carried camouflage markings, the reconnaissance versions were blue, some bright spark at the factory seemed to think that this would act as camouflage against the sky, but it still carried the now famous Royal Airforce roundels. On both side of each wing and either side of the main fuselage. This beast was built for speed, with a maximum of 409mph, because speed was its only defence, having no armament. It could outclass its main rival, the Focke Wulf FW-190.

Geary got out of the vehicle, reached into the back and pulled out his heavy sheep skin flying jacket. He proceeded to put it on as he walked the short distance over to the aircraft. He climbed aboard and his flight engineer strapped him in, making sure the straps were tight but not enough to restrict his movement. He waggled the gear stick and noticed the responses. He pushed both foot pedals, before signalling he was about to start up the engine.

He pressed the ignition and immediately the powerful Merlin 61 engine burst into life, sending flames shooting from the exhaust ports on either side of the propellor, turning it more into some mythical fire breathing dragon, than a machine of war. The propellor started to turn, getting faster and faster. Geary waved his hands, and the chocks, which kept the plane in place, were pulled away. The plane began to move, gathering speed, as he eased the throttle lever forward. He pulled the canopy over his head, securing it.

The Spitfire bumped and bobbled its way along the runway gathering pace, like a baby bird having its first flying lesson. The aircraft was a joy to fly but had its drawbacks. For one, the cockpit was set quite far back in the fuselage, that, combined with the fact that there was a huge powerful engine in front of him, limited Geary's forward view. Another issue was the landing gear set up. It made the machine very ungainly on the ground and the pilot had to fight it all the way to stop it from moving sideways. The rear wheel came off the ground and seconds later, he was airborne.

'You had to be careful on the ground because you had such a narrow undercarriage and tended to be nose heavy but once you got the aircraft into the air, it was a wonderful aircraft to fly'

F/O Peter Ayerst
No 7 Operational Training Unit

Yes, this '*bird*' was awkward on the ground but once it was in the sky, it transformed as it soared gracefully like a bird of prey. The main wheels came up into the wings and he pointed the nose of the aircraft in the direction of the Channel. He glanced down at the map, which was secured to his right leg, as he pulled his oxygen mask over his face and then looked forward, his mission clear. His mind on the job. It had to be, otherwise, he would be dead, either shot down by ground fire or by the various types of fighter aircraft that patrolled the skies, the lethal Messerschmitt BF109, the ME110, or the Focke-Wulf Fw109.

Minutes later, he was wave hopping across the Channel, keeping low, in a vain attempt not to be picked up by the enemy radar. It was turning out to be a nice day, as the sun started to rise higher in the sky, gaining strength as it did so. The mission brief was to fly as low as possible and take pictures of a chateau, that someone in Whitehall was interested in, and then, job done, get the hell out! Geary whole heartedly agreed with the last part as he pulled the stick back raising his aircraft's nose and it began to gain height.

Meanwhile, at the target, it was business as usual. The monks were wandering about doing menial tasks, as was their way, overseen by the head Abbot, who watched down on them from his office window on the third floor. A younger man in a cassock came bursting into his office.

"What is it?" Asked the Abbot without turning around.

"The coastal radar has picked up a lone aircraft heading in our direction."

"I see that scum managed to get a message through!" Hissed the Abbot. "Tell the men there is to be no shooting. Understood?" The man nodded. The Abbot looked out of the window, and over to his left, where, hidden under some camouflage netting, was an anti-aircraft battery manned by four soldiers, also dressed as monks. It was the same on the other side.

A claxon sounded a warning of the approaching aircraft, making the Abbot reach for the phone. The claxon was silenced. Other monks manned various points through the courtyard. A sudden gust of wind caught the edge of one of their cassocks, blowing it open, revealing a blue-grey uniform and an MP-40 submachine gun. The man hurriedly grabbed handfuls of material and wrapped himself up tightly, finishing off with a rope belt.

They heard the drone of the Spitfire's engine before they saw it, and then it was over them before they knew it. Many of the monks had to restrain the urge to unleash a barrage of fire on this interloper, who flew over a couple of times before disappearing the way he had come. The Abbot was pleased that their charade had not been discovered. He went over to his desk and sat down, reaching for the thick stem of a microphone.

He flicked the switch and was almost deafened by the feedback squeal.

"Brothers," he began, "once again the enemy has failed in uncovering our true intentions. It is a testimony to you, and the work that we are doing here, that we keep moving forward for our glorious leader, the Fuehrer. Sieg Heil!" He jumped to his feet and extended his right arm, the now unmistakeable Nazi salute. He could hear the others responding in a similar fashion outside, which brought him immense pleasure.

As Geary made his way home, something in the back of his mind was bothering him, like an itch he could not scratch. For the whole trip back, it gnawed at him. It was not until he made it across the English coast, and he was making his final approach to his home station, that it hit him like a punch in the face. Where was the anti-aircraft fire? The enemy fighters on the way home were obvious, in their absence. It did not sit right with him.

He had become an ace during the Battle of Britain, shooting down seven enemy aircraft, and volunteered for the hazardous reconnaissance duty, so that he could both test out and hone his skills, but this last mission was easy. Too easy. His peers would have referred to it as a milk run. However, what Geary did not know was that he had been spotted by the leader of a trio of Messerschmitt Me109s.

The leader, proudly wearing a wolf's head on a bright yellow shield on the nose of his machine, radioed that he had spotted a lone reconnaissance aircraft and that he was going in for the attack, only to be told to let it go.

He swore and looked across, first at the man on his left and then the one on his right, who both shrugged their shoulders in puzzlement.

After he touched down and parked his aircraft, Geary went straight to his commanding officer, Wing Commander Andrew '*Andy*' Crawford, and voiced his concerns. Noted, it was then passed up the line eventually landing on Forrester's desk along with the photographs. The pictures had been first sent to RAF Benson for analysis, before being sent to Forrester, accompanied by both Geary's debrief, and a report from one of the analysts at Benson. Crawford put Geary's encounter down to luck, but said he would pass the young pilot's concerns up the chain of command, which he duly did.

Seventy-two hours later, Geary's '*luck*' ran out. He was returning from a '*hop*' across the channel once more when he was bounced by three Focker Wulf FW109s. It was his own fault, really, as he was caught napping, flying straight in a combat zone. Something that had been drilled into him during training that he should never ever do.

Cannon and machine gun fire ripped through the air as Geary's plane dodged and weaved across the sky in a desperate attempt to shake off his pursuers. Lady luck would shine upon him once more. High up to his two o'clock, he saw four black dots. He cursed to himself because, he naturally assumed that his pursuers had asked for back-up. He could not have been more mistaken, as he was soon to find out.

Those dots turned out to be a squadron of Hawker Hurricane fighters and they gladly swooped down to join in on the dogfight. Geary, however, did not wait around to find out the outcome of the battle, after all, he was unarmed. When he landed, he hot footed it over to the control tower and asked for an update on the battle. The controller asked him for map references and told him that the Hurricanes had shot down two FW190s, damaged another but had lost one of their own, who had ditched in the channel.

Geary's heart sank and he turned to walk back to his barracks. The controller noticed his dejected look and asked him what was wrong. When Geary explained that he was sorry for the downed pilot's family, his heart lifted when the controller told him that the pilot had managed to bail out and had been picked up by a passing fishing boat, Geary nearly jumped for joy. He thanked the controller, headed for the nearest public house, and had a few drinks to celebrate.

According to the report submitted by RAF Benson, nothing seemed out of place. It looked like an off shoot of some kind of religious order that had been displaced because of the conflict. However, further research had failed to match up any such displacement. The report recommended further investigation. This, in conjunction with Geary's report, left the OSP commander with a decision to make.

He could order another reconnaissance flight, but that would put another pilot at risk, and he may not be as lucky as the previous one. Another option was to send in an operative, but they were like gold dust, and all of his more experience operatives were either on assignment, dead or retired. A knock came at his door.

"Enter!" He shouted as he continued to mull over in his mind what to do. The door opened, Smithers walked in, and he was not alone. A tall slim man in his early twenties, with shocking red hair, and wearing the famous green beret of a Commando, was by his side. Both men saluted. Forrester looked up and returned the salute. The stranger's face seemed strangely familiar.

"Corporal Peter Fallon reporting as requested, Sir."

"Ah. Stand easy, soldier." Forrester got to his feet and extended a hand. The two men shook. "How was your training, Fallon?"

"Tough, Sir. I didn't join a kindergarten group, so I was expecting it to be hard." It had been a year since Forrester had first clapped his eyes on the young Fallon. There was something different between the young man he saw back then, and the man standing in front of him now.

A sense of pride, of achievement. Commando training was, and still is, the toughest in the world. A year out of some young man's life during which, at any time, one slip, one mistake and that would be it. Game over. However, at the end of it, one would gain the coveted green beret, or green lid, and you would join a brotherhood. A band of brothers if you like.

"Of course." Forrester sat back down and signalled for the two men to sit. "How's your father?"

"He's fine, Sir. My mother sends her regards."

"You told them you're meeting me?" Forrester sounded worried.

"Of course!"

"How were they?"

"My mother was excited."

"And your father?"

"A bit more reserved, Sir, but that's his way."

"Been meaning to pop down for a visit but the war and stuff." Forrester admitted with a tinge of regret.

"I think they understand, Sir." Peter smiled. The radiance of it seemed to soothe the older officer sitting across from him. "Why am I here, Sir, if you don't mind me asking?"

"Not at all, young man." Forrester's fatherly tone kicked in, "I need to send someone over to France to investigate a little mystery."

"And you want me to do this, Sir?"

"Yes." Forrester stretched over, lifted a file from the top of his 'In' tray, and opened it. He fell silent for a few minutes as he studied the contents before closing it in such a way, it added a kind of finality to the gesture. "According to your file, you have scored extremely well in both your basic and advanced commando training. Your instructors speak very highly of you."

"Thank you, Sir."

"I'm only relaying what they say, Corporal. Your SOE instructors were similarly impressed but I see there is a blemish on this report." He paused, and looked across at Fallon, a sternness appearing on his face. "You hit an officer."

"Yes, Sir. I did." Admitted Fallon. Forrester studied the young man in front of him, looking for any sign of weakness or regret. He found none.

"Care to explain?"

"The officer in question had had a bit too much to drink and he made improper advances towards one of the WAAFs (Women's Auxiliary Airforce) whilst we were doing our signalling training at Bletchley Park."

"And?"

"I stepped in, Sir."

"You stepped in..." Repeated Forrester whose eyes darted between Fallon and Smithers and back again. Smithers just sat there with a huge smile on his face. An eyebrow raise from Forrester made it disappear, because he knew what his adjutant was thinking, the reason for the smile – like father, like son.

"Yes, Sir. The officer's conduct was unbecoming, and I asked him to leave the young lady alone."

"And what was his response?"

"He tried to hit me."

"Is that when you punched him?"

"No, Sir. I managed to dodge the blow. It was when he used some ungentlemanly language towards the young lady that I decked him with one punch."

"Ah." Forrester got to his feet and walked over to his office window. He stood there for a moment looking out, allowing the young NCO to stew for the duration before turning to face him. "Lucky for you, the young lady backed up your story, otherwise, you would be heading for the stockade rather than sitting here in my office."

"I detest bullies, Sir."

"Don't we all, Corporal. There's a certain bully across the Channel called Adolph Hitler, who's causing our office some problems and we've been tasked with sorting him out. Interested in giving us a hand?" Forrester extended his hand again, but the intention was different from the first time.

Then, it was a welcome, this time it was to affirm his compliance. Without thinking, Fallon jumped to his feet and took the hand, shaking it so enthusiastically, Forrester had to raise his other hand to make him release.

"Sorry, Sir." Fallon apologised.

"Think nothing of it, Lieutenant Fallon."

"I'm sorry, Sir but I think you've got that wrong." Said Fallon pointing to the stripes on his arm.

"No, you've got it wrong, Lieutenant. You see, people who work for the Office of Special Projects can only be officers. Think of it like the membership of an exclusive club, and you have just taken out a membership."

"Thank you, Sir."

"One more thing…." Added Forrester as Fallon and Smithers got up to leave.

"Sir?"

"From now on, you will be referred to as K-12."

"Just like my father." Fallon's face beamed with pride.

"Exactly." Forrester went across to the window and looked out. This part of the mission was done, "dismissed!"

5 – Altman

A shout went out from one of the sentries. The Abbot looked out of his window and saw a cloud of dust in the distance. He immediately reached for his telephone and contacted the main sentry box.

"Yes?" Asked the sentry.

"What is the cause of the dust cloud? Can you see?"

"Yes, Sir. It is a convoy, but none is expected."

"Go to amber alert!" Ordered the Abbot.

"Immediately, Sir."

The sentry shouted an order into a small shack situated next to the box, and several soldiers came running out, taking up positions behind piles of sandbags sheltering under netting. One of each group pulled a tarpaulin off a hump in the middle of the semi-circle formed by the sandbags, revealing a Mauser MG-34 machine gun.

He opened the top of the weapon, fed in a belt of bullets, as if he were feeding some kind of monster, and slammed the top down, pulling back the firing pin and aiming it down the road, as did his opposite number in the other machine gun nest. The sound of engines was clearer now, and the dust began to settle revealing two motorcycle outriders, complete with sidecars, a Kubelwagen staff car behind, followed by two tarpaulin covered Opel trucks and another two motorcycles at the rear.

The convoy stopped at the machine gun nests and one of the sentries came forward with his MP-40 machine gun dangling over his shoulder. He came up to the Kubelwagen. The occupants were an NCO in the front, driving and two men in the back. He recognised the rank of the officer as a Generaloberst, or General, the other man was a civilian. He saluted the General and asked for his identification papers. The officer flashed his ID card, as did the civilian. The officer was Manfred Altman.

"Open the gate!" Ordered the General.

"Are you expected Sir?" Asked the Sentry.

"Do you like the food here, Corporal?" Came the snippy reply.

"Yes Sir."

"If you don't open the gate, you will be sampling the food somewhere less pleasant!"

"Immediately, Sir!" The sentry signalled for the bar across the road to be raised and he saluted as the convoy passed him. The two front outriders peeled off as the staff car stopped outside the front entrance of the chateau. The Abbot stood at the top of the steps and slowly came down. The NCO opened the passenger door, flipped the front seat forward and the two passengers got out.

The Abbot saluted the General, who returned the salute. The civilian did not salute but just stood there with his hands behind his back. The Abbot was taken aback by the rudeness of the civilian but stifled his emotions.

"To what do I owe this visit, Herr General?" Inquired the Abbot motioning them inside.

"I am to take over your operation here."

"But Sir...!" Protested the Abbot.

"Orders from the Fuhrer himself." The General handed the Abbot an official looking envelope. He opened it and on headed note paper from the Reich Chancellery, was a letter ordering him to relinquish command and signed by Adolph Hitler. The Abbot sighed but resigned to the fact he was being replaced.

"A drink?" Offered the Abbot as they entered the main hall. The General nodded but the civilian raised his hand in abstention. "Cognac?"

"That would be sufficient to wash away the taste of these inferior French roads." Said the officer dusting himself off with his gloves before sitting down.

"Can I ask who you're travelling companion is, Herr General?"

"How rude of me. This is Herr Doktor Pieter Titus." Titus nodded slightly but remained quiet.

"Can I ask one more question?"

"Go ahead." The General took a sip of the Cognac and smiled with satisfaction.

"Why are you here? The letter only goes as far as telling me you are replacing me, but nothing about the reason for it. Have I failed the Fuhrer and the Reich?"

"The reason, I'm afraid, is classified but you have not failed, Herr Abbot. In fact, the Fuhrer is very pleased with your work here and has request your presence back in Berlin. You leave tomorrow."

"I am honoured, Herr General."

It was then that the three men became aware of a Hauptmann, or Captain, standing in the doorway, when he coughed politely.

"What is it, Schuman?" Asked the General.

"The crates are ready to be unloaded, Sir. Where shall we store them?"

"Ah, good. Herr Abbot?"

"Err. They can be transferred to the cellar via the entrance at the side of the building. If you will excuse me, gentlemen." The General gave his permission and the Abbot left with the Captain.

"This is very good Cognac, Herr Doktor. You don't know what you're missing."

"I do not drink that filth, Herr General!" Hissed Titus.

"Come, come Titus. Live a little." Mocked the General taking another sip and easing himself deeper into the chair, crossing his legs. He gave out a sigh of contentment. Since being given this assignment, he had had little time to relax. The organisation required for this project had been both immense and time consuming. Many long nights burning the midnight oil in conferences with other officers and the Fuhrer himself.

He reached down, and picked up a brown leather satchel, that he had placed there when he had sat down, placing it across his lap, he clicked back the two latches and opened it, pulling out a brown folder with a large German eagle stamped across the front. He opened it and began to refresh his memory concerning '*Operation Storm.*' Titus squirmed uneasily in his chair making the General look up.

"May I be excused to supervise the unloading, Herr General? The equipment is very delicate, and I don't trust those animals under your command to treat it with either the delicacy or respect it requires." The General dismissed him with a wave of his hand.

Several hours had gone by from the time the General and his men had arrived, which had allowed him to move into the chateau. His belongings had been moved into the main room on the first floor and the Abbot's stuff had been packed ready for his departure in a few hours. The officer stood behind what had once been the Abbot's desk surveying various reports and maps when the telephone rang. He picked it up.

"Yes?"

"It is a call from the Fuhrer's office, Herr General." Informed the switchboard.

"Danke." Thanked the General as he straightened himself up, pulling down the corners of his tunic, like some first year cadet attending his first parade. It was silly, he knew this because he would be speaking to his superior on the telephone and not in person, but his superior oozed both fear and respect in equal measures. To offend the Fuhrer was to send a death nail into your career and even your life. The line clicked a couple of times before a female voice came on the other end.

"Hold for the Fuhrer."

"Altman?" Came a man's voice after a short pause.

"Yes, Mein Fuhrer."

"How are the preparations for Operation Storm coming?"

"We have just arrived, Mein Fuhrer, and are proceeding with setting the equipment up."

"Good. Very Good. Keep me informed. The Reich is depending upon your success." The line went dead before Altman could reply. He replaced the handset and stood there beaming, like a schoolboy who has just been given his favourite sweet as a reward for good behaviour.

Three hours later, the Kubelwagen containing the Abbot, drove out of the main gate just as a lorry came up the road. The two vehicles passed each other allowing the Abbot to see that the lorry was carrying several more civilians in the back, making him wonder what the hell they were doing at the chateau. He had spent twelve months setting up the cover story they had lived, eaten, and slept only once it was established to be tossed aside like some unwanted pet.

Inside he was seething but he dared not show his anger. He had been summoned to Berlin, so hopefully he would find out what was going on when he got there. The journey to the German capital was going to be long, he sat back and let his mind drift off. His work here was done.

"The other scientists have arrived, Herr General." Informed Schuman.

"Good. Have them billeted and ask the Herr doktor to join me."

"At once, Sir."

"You asked to see me, General?" Asked Titus as he stood in the doorway five minutes later.

"Yes, sit."

"I prefer to stand."

"Suit yourself. I've just had a conversation with the Fuhrer, and he is very pleased with our progress."

"As he should be."

"Your arrogance is both impressive and annoying, Titus!"

"When you have to lower yourself to work with inferiors, arrogance is my only shield against becoming a lesser being."

"Jesus! You are full of it, aren't you!" Cursed Altman, "may I remind you, you arrogant bastard, that a bullet can kill you, just as much as it can us lesser mortals, and that's what will happen to us if we fail."

"Then, there is only one option."

"And that is?"

"We will not fail."

Altman shook his head in disbelief before continuing, "do we have an update?"

"Yes. The rest of my team have arrived, and the equipment has been unloaded. It will take a few days for it all to be checked and recalibrated. The journey has misaligned some of the dials."

"How long is a couple of days?"

"As long as it takes to do the necessary work, General. Excellence cannot be rushed." And with that, he left leaving Altman speechless.

6 – K-12

Whilst all this was going on across the Channel, Fallon had received both his transfer orders to the Office of Special Projects and his accelerated promotion to Lieutenant. The two pips on his lapels did not feel right. He felt a fraud for not gaining them the right way, but it still felt good as he entered the front door of OSP headquarters when both a Sergeant and a Corporal both saluted him in rapid fashion. He climbed the stairs to the third floor, where Forrester's office was situated. He paused, outside a room with the number '*007*' on it before knocking. Smithers opened it and smiled.

"It suits you, old chap." He said referring to the two pips.

"It feels wrong, Sir." Confessed Fallon as he entered the outer sanctum.

"Sir?" Repeated Smithers quizzically and then he remembered that according to normal military etiquette, he outranked Fallon. "Ah. About that," he continued, "at the OSP, the only person we referred to as 'Sir' is the man behind that big oak door. I'm just Smithers or K-14 and you're Fallon or K-12."

"Got it, Sir. I mean Smithers." Replied Fallon a little uneasy. "It's going to take a bit of getting used to."

"Agreed, but you'll eventually get the idea. I was in the same boat when I first met your father back in Cairo. Only then, the roles were reversed. If you would follow me, please, K-12." Smithers went to the aforementioned oak door and knocked hard on it. There was a stifled sound from within and Smithers paused for a moment before entering. "K-12 is here, Sir."

"Jolly good. Send him in."

Fallon entered and found Forrester sitting at his desk smoking his pipe looking over some files. He approached the desk and stood at attention. Forrester looked up at him and dismissed the formality with a wave of his hand before pointing to an empty chair.

"How do you feel, K-12?" Asked Forrester without looking up from the file.

"Depends on what you mean, Sir?"

"Are you fitting in alright?"

"It's a bit awkward, Sir but according to Smithers, I'll cope."

"Smithers? Not Captain Smithers?" Queried the officer, then he smiled. "I see he has given you the talk."

"The talk, Sir?"

"About how we refer to each other in this department."

"Yes Sir."

"How did he refer to me this time? Him behind the oak door or the old man?"

"The man behind the oak door, Sir."

"Ah." Again, Forrester smiled a knowing smile. "Smithers and I have been together for a very long time, Lieutenant." He explained, "he is the only one I would allow to get away with calling me the old man…"

"Understood, Sir."

For the first time since Fallon had arrived, Forrester looked across at him and shook his head disapprovingly, clicking his tongue on the roof of his mouth as he did so. "That will not do!" He reached over and pressed his intercom. Smithers entered. "K-12's hair colour just won't do, Smithers. Kindly do something about it, be a good chap."

"Yes, Sir."

"I think blonde would suit."

"Agreed." Replied Smithers almost shooing Fallon out of the office.

"Dismissed." Forrester added as an afterthought. He looked up and found himself alone. He shook his head and then returned to his pipe and the file. A few hours later, after a trip to a barbers, the new look 'blonde' haired Fallon and Smithers were descending the stairs into the bowels of the earth, searching out the armoury officer, Gerald Cuthbertson, or 'Sparks', to his colleagues.

A genius in his own mind and a master of invention. They eventually found him beavering away at a work bench whilst several other white coated individuals worked at other benches scattered through the basement. The smell of gunpowder heavy in the air. Smithers approached Cuthbertson from behind and tapped him on the shoulder. The man almost jumped out of his skin in fright.

"Jesus, Mary, and Joseph!" He cursed holding a hand on his chest. "How many times have I told you not to do that?"

"I've lost count." Replied Smithers laughing. "Sparks. Fallon. Fallon. Sparks." He introduced.

"Ah yes. The new K-12 I've heard about." He extended a hand. The two men shook. "Pleased to finally meet you."

"Likewise. My father has told me a lot about you."

"Your father?" Cuthbertson looked over to Smithers with a puzzled look on his face.

"This is Jonathan Fallon's son."

"Little Peter?" Smithers nodded. "No bloody way! It seems like only yesterday that I was bouncing him on my knee."

"Pleased to meet you again, Uncle Sparks."

"You'll have to forgive me, Peter, but when Smithers, said your surname, it didn't click."

"I think someone's been down here too long." Suggested Smithers.

"Anyway!" Cuthbertson dismissed the insinuation and turned back to his workbench. "Here's what I have been working on." He opened his hands about shoulder width apart to almost frame a tatty looking, small suitcase.

"You do know, you can pick up a new one in the High Street, Sparks?" Quipped Smithers.

"Ignore him, K-12." He shot Smithers a sideways glance before carrying on, "it looks like and behaves like an old fashioned suitcase. The kind one would take on an overnight stay. Correct?" Fallon nodded. "Click the latches when they are in the perpendicular position and the case opens…"

Click! Click! The lid opened revealing an empty case. Cuthbertson closed the lid, fastening the locks. "Now, turn the latches horizontal and open…" Click! Click! The lid sprung open like the last time but this time there was a small radio inside, as well as a passport, and a couple of clips of ammunition. "Remember, it is vital important that the latches are facing West to East and not the other way around."

"Why is that? What will happen?" Asked Fallon.

"If you place the latches facing East to West and try to unlock it, it will detonate a small explosive device, thus destroying the contents and probably causing serious harm to the person opening it."

"So, if they tried to rob you, their ideas will blow up in their face? Is that what you're trying to tell us, Sparks?" Asked Smithers, his tongue very firmly in his cheek.

"Your playground antics are wasted on me, Smithers." Chastised Cuthbertson rolling his eyes. He walked over to another bench where one of his colleagues had just finished working on a uniform. He held it up as equipment officer approached.

"Ready, Mister Cuthbertson."

"Very good, Jeffrey. Very good indeed." Cuthbertson summoned Fallon over. On closer inspection, the uniform bore the rank insignia of a German army Major. "Be very careful when you button the tunic up as the third button from the top is actually a small explosive, which only has a twenty second fuse."

"How is it activated?" Asked Fallon.

"When you pull it off the garment, it's like pulling the pin on a grenade, except this has enough explosive power to knock a sizeable hole in a brick wall. The bottom button is a homing device which is turned on in the similar way to the explosive. It is also magnetic which means you can attach it to something and track it via your new watch."

Right on cue, another white coated technician appeared at his side and handed him an ordinary looking watch. The kind you could easily get in one of the frequent open air markets you used to get in German villages before the war. "Turn the outer dial of the watch one complete turn clockwise and the little jewel at the six o'clock position will act as your guide. The stronger the flash, the nearer you are to the button."

"Very impressive. You should work in the motion picture industry after the war. I'm sure someone in their special effects department could use someone with the imagination you've got, Sparks." Commented Smithers.

"Actually, an American film company has already approached me."

"Oh. And what did you tell them?"

"I politely declined saying that my country needed me more."

"Quite right. Well done old man!" Congratulated Smithers, patting Cuthbertson on the back. A look of downright hostility shot across Cuthbertson's face at this gesture. Smithers seemed to crumble slightly under this gaze and quickly withdrew his hand.

"At the moment, your personal side arm will be the Webley Mark Three. It has a shorter barrel than the Mark One, making it easier to conceal. However, once you get to your destination, you will be using the Walther PPK. The standard side arm of an officer of your rank. Please don't get the two mixed up as the consequences could be disastrous."

"Thanks. I'll try and remember that." Fallon took the uniform and went across to the first bench. He turned the latches so that they were facing up and down. Click! Click! The lid opened revealing the empty case. He placed the uniform inside. Sparks joined him.

"The final part of the charade are your papers. Travel orders signed by your regimental commander, your identification papers, and pictures of a non-existent family. You must read the enclosed documents and render them to memory. If you are caught, your memory may be your only chance of survival. I've also included seven hundred francs in this envelope. Spending money if you like." The papers and envelope went on top of the uniform. Finally, Cuthbertson handed him a peaked officer's cap which sat nicely on the stack before he closed the lid. "Good luck, K-12."

"Thanks." The two men shook, and Fallon turned to leave.

"Please come back alive." Added Cuthbertson.

"I'll do my very best." Replied Fallon flashing a faint smile before leaving.

"Does he have a chance, Smithers?" Asked a worried Cuthbertson.

"About as much as any of us, old chap. About as much as any of us." Replied Smithers watching the young man climb the stairs.

They headed back to Forrester's office for the final briefing before departure. They found him standing looking at a map pinned on the wall. He was deep in thought studying it when they knocked and walked in. He was reviewing pictures from the Spitfire fly-by again and Forrester looked perplexed. He tossed them on his desk in frustration.

"Nothing. Absolutely nothing!" He said looking at his two subordinates. "Anything to add?" Smithers picked up the pictures and looked at each one before passing them to Fallon. Both shook their heads. "So, why the hell would Sparrowhawk risk blowing his cover over nothing?"

"Guess I'll need to take a look, Sir." Suggested Fallon tapping his suitcase.

Forrester nodded and then added, "there's a Lysander aircraft making a routine drop to a local Maquis unit in the area. I've managed to book you a seat. Your mission is reconnaissance only, K-12. Don't engage the enemy. Return to base and then we'll take it from there. Understood?"

"Yes Sir." Fallon saluted but slowly took his hand down under a frown from Forrester. He turned and left.

"You know, I really wish he would stop doing that." Commented Forrester.

"Was I that green when I joined, Sir?" Asked Smithers.

"Worse, but at least you had time to acclimatise. He doesn't."

"God help him."

"God may not be what he needs right now, Smithers." Smithers looked over at him puzzled, "he needs luck more than divine intervention."

7 – The Fake Major

The journey, via staff car, took twenty minutes out to the airfield where the Lysander Mark IIIA of number six-one-six squadron was waiting, its engine already turning over. Its Bristol Mercury air-cooled engine looked and sounded impressive. The aircraft itself looked more like an ugly duckling than a swan, with its high wings and a fixed, non-retractable landing gear which was mounted on an innovative inverted U square-section tube that supported wings struts at the apex and contained internal springs for the flared wheels.

The large, streamlined spats, or housings, also contained a mounting for a Browning machine gun and fittings for removeable stub wings that could carry light bombs or supply cannisters.

The wings had a reverse taper towards the body of the aircraft, which gave the impression of a bent gull wing from some angles, although the spars were straight. It had a girder type construction faired with a light wood stringer to give the aerodynamic shape. The forward fuselage was duralumin tube joined with brackets and plates, and the after part was welded stainless steel tubes. Plates and brackets were cut from channel extrusions rather than being well formed from sheet steel. Despite its appearance, the aircraft had built up quite a reputation for being both reliable and being able to take a lot of punishment.

Its short take-off and landing capabilities made it ideal for the covert operations it was being used for. Its livery was black with toned down RAF roundels. Fallon could see under the main fuselage; a couple of ground crew were tinkering with some kind of torpedo shaped pod. As he approached, the pilot looked over briefly before returning to speaking to the ground crew, him standing there with his hands on his hips.

The staff car stopped a few feet away and Fallon got out. He waved the car off before approaching. The pilot turned once more and looked none too pleased.

"So, you're the so-and-so I've been held back for, huh?"

"I'm afraid so." Fallon extended a hand but found nothing in return but an annoyed look. "The name's Serpens. Louis Serpens."

"Not interested, mate. I'm just the taxi driver. Get aboard." The dismissive nature exhibited by the pilot irritated Fallon, such disrespect aimed at a superior officer was intolerable. He made a mental note to report the pilot once he returned.

Fallon climbed into the rear cockpit; it was a tight squeeze. "Don't I get a parachute or something?"

He asked, commenting about the sparseness of his current predicament.

"Why? If we get shot at, our arses will hit the floor quicker than if you had jumped with a parachute." The pilot had a final conversation with the ground crew before climbing into the front of the aircraft. He signalled for Fallon to pull his half of the canopy forward just as he pushed the accelerator stick forward and the aircraft lurched forward. The click of the canopy had a finality to it and made Fallon a little uneasy.

Meanwhile, across the Channel, six men stood in an 'L' shape, under the instruction of a tall dark haired woman, wearing a black heavy coat and a Sten gun Mark II slung over her shoulder. She used a mixture of whispers and hand movements, like a choreographer directing her dancers, to get the men into the right position.

The group would freeze on the spot if an owl hooted, or a twig snapped. She was relying on her spotters further up the lane to alert her about oncoming traffic both friendly and hostile. Three other men covered her and the group, from the thicket, each carrying Sten guns. It was a clear night. The clouds were caressing the moon as they passed in front of it.

Clear, but there was a bite in the wind that danced across the field. They paused and listened for the distinct sound of the Lysander's engine. She was no rookie and had done this many times but each time she did it, lessened her chances of escape, and increased the percentages of being caught by a random patrol. A bird screeched as it took to the air, causing the group to freeze, and then hit the ground, hugging it for dear life.

Eyes scanning the darkness looking for the slightest movement. False alarm. And then they heard it, a low drone to begin with off to the West but getting louder. She signalled to the half dozen men in the field to stand up, each man raising a lantern skyward. She looked at her watch and decided to give them three minutes to see their signal and land.

This was when their exposure was at its greatest. Everyone would be watching the dark hulking brute of an aircraft rather than their assigned jobs. She gave out a low whistle, directed at one of the men in the thicket, and used her first two fingers to signal to him to concentrate on watching the road. He nodded; she rolled her eyes.

Since taking over the group after Sparrowhawk had been killed, she had personally lost four good friends. Two killed and two captured by the dreaded Gestapo, the head of which was a man called Frettchen. The locals called him 'the Weasel' because of his thin elongated looks and pronounced pointed nose, similar to the animal in question.

The Geheime Staatspolizei (Secret State Police) was the official secret police of Nazi Germany and in German occupied Europe. Created by Herman Goring in 1933, by combining the various political police agencies of Prussia into one organisation.

On 20th April 1934, oversight of the Gestapo passed to the head of the Schutzstaffel (SS), Heinrich Himmler, who was also appointed Chief of Police by Adolf Hitler *in 1936. Instead of being exclusively a Prussian state agency, the Gestapo became a national one as a sub-office of the Sicherheitspolizei (SiPo; Security Police).*

From 27th September 1939, the Riech Security Main Office (RSHA) administered it. It became known as Amt (Dept) 4 of the RSHA and was considered a sister organisation to the Sicherheitdienst (SD; Security Service).

Frettchen was an evil man, taking great delight in the suffering of his captives. He wore the standard knee length black leather coat and fedora hat, but he walked with the aid of a cane with the handle in the shape of a wolf's head. He also had a scar on his left cheek. Gossip mongers amongst his subordinates were split in the origin of this. Some said it was a duelling scar, but others suggested it was from the husband of one of his many mistresses, for Frettchen considered himself somewhat of a ladies man.

He never went very far without his henchman, a hulking bald-headed brute called Wiesel. A Schutzstaffel, or SS, Sergeant with a similar taste for brutality his master had. It was said that Wiesel kept a diary of all the victims he had interrogated, rating his performance on a scale of one to ten, with the higher end of the scale being the most brutal. On his left upper arm, he had a deaths head tattoo and the motto of the SS – '*Meine Here Heisst Treue*' – '*My Honour is Loyalty.*' They made a couple from your worst nightmare.

The plane waggled its wings as it came into land, bouncing just once before its wheels connected with terra firma before the engine was flung into reverse, the flaps down and the brakes applied. It was a quick change over. A man from the woods hurried forwards as Fallon climbed out and plonked himself onto the grass. The woman ran forward shook his hand briefly before ushering him into the safety of the thicket, whilst back at the plane, her men released the latch on the pod, retrieved the ammo and weapons, and then resealing it allowing the plane to turn around and take-off again.

All done in around five minutes. Pretty impressive operation, Fallon thought as he was guided to a waiting truck. He climbed in the back along with two of the group, the woman and another man got in up front. The man at the tail gate reached up and pulled the tarpaulin down covering the exit. They took the lesser known back roads in an effort to avoid the patrols and eventually stopped at a barn. The woman got out and opened the double doors, then marshalled the truck inside before closing the doors. The tarp went up and the men jumped down. One lit a lantern, placing it on top of an upturned packing case.

"Welcome, Monsieur. I am Dianne."

"Louis."

"London has briefed us on why you're here, and we have been ordered to help you as much as we can."

"That would be most helpful, Dianne." Thanked Fallon putting down his suitcase.

"Is that all you have?" She asked, disappointed.

"It's all I need. Do you have the transport London requested?"

"Oui, follow me." She took him to the back of the barn where a large bulge was concealed by a sheet.

With the help of her men, the sheet was lifted off, revealing a Kubelwagen.

"May I ask where you got this?"

"We liberated it from a fat General, my friend!" Said a large moustache man leaning against the truck, "don't worry. He won't be needing it any time soon." He drew his thumb across his throat from ear to ear before erupting into an enormous belly laugh.

"Will there be repercussions?"

"Probably." Replied Dianne, almost shrugging it off, "that is the way we live here. Some live. Some die." She said this with such coldness that Fallon actually felt pity for her. The woman was very beautiful, but she had an aura of danger about her. An edginess. Fallon wondered what terrible things she had witnessed to turn her into what she had become. That warmth of a woman of her age should have had been snuffed out like a campfire that had out lasted its use.

"Is there somewhere I can change?" Fallon asked.

"In the stall at the end, pretty boy!" Laughed the big man with the moustache. Fallon thanked Dianne and went to get changed, emerging moments later in his Wehrmacht Major's uniform. There was a stunned silence as he put his cap on his head.

"Major Conrad Schlange. At your service, fraulein." He clicked his heels together and gave her a slight nod. Dianne smiled briefly and then it was gone like a whisp of smoke.

"Very impressive, Monsieur. This is Phillippe. He will be your driver." A small man wearing a Wehrmacht Corporal's uniform stepped forward and saluted him.

Fallon rummaged in his case, taking out his sidearm, the Walther, and his watch, strapping it to his right wrist.

"I like your watch, Monsieur." Commented the moustache man.

"You can have it when I'm dead." Replied Fallon.

"Soon then, huh?" Moustached man suggested and then laughed again.

Fallon tossed his suitcase in the boot and the map of the area on the backseat before flipping back the front seat, getting in the back. Phillippe closed the door and went around, getting into the driver's side.

"Bon chance, mes amis." Wished Dianne as she signalled for the barn doors to be opened. She waved them goodbye as the car sped off into the darkness.

It was seven o'clock and the rooster had crowed an hour or so ago, as the Kubelwagen containing Phillippe and Fallon appeared around the corner of the approach road to the chateau. The sound of its washing machine like engine attracted attention from the guards further up the road. The Captain of the guard shouted for someone to man one of the machine gun nests, keeping the arrivals covered as they came closer.

"Easy, Phillippe. Easy." Soothed Fallon from the back seat.

"Oui, Monsieur...err... I mean, yes, Herr Major."

The car came to a halt and the Captain of the guard came forward.

"Papers!" He demanded.

"Are you blind, Sergeant?" Asked Fallon tersely.

"No, why do you ask?"

"Is that anyway to speak to a superior officer or perhaps a trip to the Russian Front will sharpen your eye?" Threatened Fallon.

Immediately, the Sergeant saw the error of his ways and came to a stiff attention, saluting the Major. "My apologies, Sir. Can I have your papers please." Grovelled the Sergeant. Fallon was now relishing the role and slowly took off his brown leather gloves before reaching into his jacket pocket and handing over his identification. "Major Schlange. I am afraid I don't have you on my visitors list."

"And neither you shall, Sergeant. I am from Army Group Seven, and I am scouting around the nearby chateaus looking for suitable lodgings for the officers under my command..."

"But Sir. I am afraid there has been some kind of mistake."

"Mistake?"

"Yes Sir. This area is under the command of General Manfred Altman, of the Special Projects Division."

"Altman? Altman?" Repeated Fallon pretending to try and remember the name, "do we know an Altman, Hans?" Phillippe leaned back and shook his head. His nerves had gone, and he too, like Fallon, was beginning to enjoy himself in the role.

"The General is under orders from the Fuhrer himself."

"Ah, that explains it." Said Fallon retrieving his papers and putting his gloves back on.

"Explains what, Herr Major?"

"It has been sometime since I was back in Berlin and have lost touch with the Fuhrer's grand schemes."

"But Sir...!" Argued the Sergeant.

"Radio ahead and tell the General that we're coming, if you would be so kind." The Sergeant opened his mouth to protest again, but thought better of it, as Fallon shooed him away with a couple of flicks of his hand. The Sergeant disappeared into the guard post returning after a brief telephone conversation.

"Raise the gate." He ordered and the red and white barrier was raised. The Kubelwagen trundled forwards towards the chateau.

"I think, the Major enjoyed that." Whispered Phillippe once they were out of earshot.

"You would be right." Laughed Fallon. As they came towards the large impressive looking building, Fallon noticed a couple of lorries parked off to the side, one of which had its tarpaulin raised revealing several barrels with a skull and crossbones stencilled on the side. He made a mental note to ask his host about them when they met. He also noticed that, apart from the guards they had met at the entrance, everyone else was wearing monks robes. Another puzzling thing to raise, perhaps?

The car stopped, and Phillippe opened the door as Fallon flipped the front seat. He got out and whispered to the Frenchman to be on his guard. The Frenchman whispered back that he would be and wished the Major 'good hunting.' As Fallon climbed the stairs, Phillippe got into the car and did a circuit of the courtyard before parking it next to the trucks. He noticed a couple of the drivers were sitting out on fold-up chairs chewing the fat with each other. He jumped on the opportunity to gather some information.

"Can I join you?" He asked pointing to a vacant chair.

"Yes. Where are you from?" Asked one of the drivers, a Corporal, like Phillippe.

"Army Group Seven, down here with my Major, scouting for billets for the rest of the privileged assholes."

"I hear you, brother." Agreed the Corporal.

"Why are you here?" Asked Phillippe.

"Transport duty for the General."

"What are you transporting?"

The Corporal was about to reply when his colleague coughed and shook his head. "I'm sorry friend, but I can't answer that."

"Fair enough." Conceded Phillippe pulling out a packet of cheap cigarettes from his breast pocket and offered them around. The three men sat around for the next hour chatting about this and that. Nothing in particular. All the while, Phillippe looked around watching the comings and goings. Why were their men in strange, rubberised suits and gas masks coming in and out of that low roof building to the rear of the chateau? He decided, there and then, that further investigation was needed. He excused himself for a toilet break, and one of them was kind enough to give him directions.

Phillippe started off in the direction given but darted behind a truck when he was sure he was not being watched. Before leaving the barn, Fallon had given him a small camera on the strict instructions to gather as much intel as possible without putting their primary mission into jeopardy.

He checked around him one final time before climbing into the back of one of the trucks. To his dismay, it was empty except for a label that must have fallen off one of the barrels the suited men were wielding into the low roofed building. It was yellow with a skull and crossbones on it, above which was printed 'LD-27'. Click, went the camera. He decided to take a picture of the interior of the truck too in case it provided the smart people in intelligence some clues as to what was being moved. He carefully lifted a corner of the tarpaulin, no-one about, so he dropped back down to the ground and re-joined his friends.

"Cognac, Major?" Offered Altman.

"Yes Sir. Thank you." Fallon took the glass and sat down on one of the numerous plush chairs. Altman sat opposite, studying him with a critical eye.

"You look very young to be a Major."

"Very true, Sir. I was stationed on the Eastern Front, and most of my unit was wiped out, including the officers, headquarters had to scrape the bottom of the barrel, so to speak, and you see the result." Fallon used a wide sweeping movement over himself, a gesture in self-mockery, a deflection, if you like. The General paused and then laughed. Fallon thought it prudent to join him. Then they realised they were not alone. Both men turned to see a man dressed in a knee length leather coat and black fedora, it was Frettchen.

"Heil Hitler!" He shouted extending his arm. The two officers jumped to their feet.

"Heil Hitler!"

"Major Schlange, this is Interrogator Frettchen of the Gestapo." Introduced Altman. Both men nodded in the other's direction.

"I trust I've not been keeping you waiting, Herr General?"

"No. The Major was a pleasant distraction."

"Which unit do you belong to, Herr Major?"

"Army Group Seven."

"Strange. I have received no notification your unit was anywhere near here."

"I'm on a scouting trip looking for billets in the area, for our ranking officers."

"Ah-so."

"Sweet mother! Is that the time?" Said Fallon pretending to look at his watch, "my General will be wondering where I've got to. Gentlemen, it has been a pleasure." Fallon saluted and made a hasty retreat down the steps. He waved at Phillippe to bring the car forward. Once in the car, he told Phillippe to hastily make an exit but in such a way not to draw suspicion. Too late. Back in the chateau, Frettchen was already on the telephone to his office in the nearby town asking for a direct line to the headquarters of Army Group Seven. After a heated conversation with someone on the other end of the phone, he slammed the receiver down.

"What is it?" Asked Altman.

"Army Group Seven is currently on manoeuvres in the North of the country. That was their personnel officer. They have no trace of a Major Schlange." Altman grabbed the phone and buzzed the front gate ordering the two men detained that had just left the main house. He too slammed down the telephone.

"It's too late. They're gone."

A couple of miles down the road from the chateau, two locals stood next to a German staff car laughing. The blonde haired one took one look at the car, before lighting the rag that was sticking out of the petrol tank, and then the two of them together, with one mighty shove, pushed the car over the ravine. They stood watching it bounce and jump a couple of times before it burst into flames ending in a blazing heap at the bottom. They congratulated each other before walking off down the country lane towards a distant farmhouse and barn, their mission complete.

8 – Closeness

Once the two men had managed to get to the farmhouse, Fallon went inside to speak to Dianne to arrange for a pick-up. Phillippe returned to the barn and took great delight recounting their brush with the Germans over a glass or three of cheap red wine. After a brief radio message was exchanged with headquarters, a pick-up was arranged for that night, ten hours away. Fallon had time to burn.

"What do French people do when they have nothing but time?" Fallon asked.

"We walk, we drink, we eat, and we make love."

"Do we have to do it in that order?" Smiled Fallon.

"It is easier." Said Dianne pulling a knitted black shawl off the back of the door and wrapping it around her head.

"Okay then. A walk it is." Relented Fallon following her out into the courtyard. The sun was at its highest, beaming down warmth and happiness onto everything it could reach. Birds were singing and children were playing. Ducks played in a nearby pond. Tranquillity at its very best. You would hardly believe there was a war on. In this part of France, the locals were allowed to carry on with as much of their normal life as possible under the ever watchful eye of the occupying Germans.

Marquis attacks were minimal unlike other regions, not that the local resistance was not around, far from it. They were everywhere but knew when to strike and when to wait. They calculated. Gathering information and passing them back to the Allies. In fact, the last piece of excitement was the Sparrowhawk affair.

The tranquillity acted like a drug on Fallon and Dianne as they walked. As it progressed, the two of them got closer as they talked about trivial things like what they would do after the war if the Allies won, if either were married, the scenery and the weather. Eventually, Dianne's hand brushed gently against Fallon's. At first, he ignored it, and continued to walk but when it happened a second time, he turned and looked at her. Him into her brown eyes and her into his blue.

The conversation stopped, and they just stood there looking at each other, wondering what the other was thinking and what the next move would be. Fallon was the first to move, he turned and started to walk ahead leaving Dianne to catch up. They climbed over a wooden style that led to a meadow, full of yellow and white flowers, which moved silently with the breeze, releasing a pleasant cleansing fragrance into the air. She got alongside him and playfully pushed him, giggled like a schoolgirl before running off ahead. Fallon gave chase and eventually caught her returning the shove which sent her sprawling forwards. She hit the ground on her stomach and lay there without moving.

Thinking he had injured her, Fallon rushed forward and knelt down beside her, placing his hands on her shoulders and turning her over so she was in the supine position, face up. She still did not move. He bent down to check her pulse and to listen for breathing. It was then, he realised, she had been playing possum when she kissed him fully on the lips. At first, Fallon drew back caught off guard. She looked up at him with a look of embarrassment. His face poker straight.

"I am sorry." She apologised before trying to get to her feet. Fallon pushed her back down and his poker face smashed into a broad smile.

"Two can play possum, you know." He said and came in close. They kissed. Their bodies pressing against each other as the power of romance, or perhaps lust, encapsulated them, whisking them away, allowing them to forget, even for the briefest of moments, the dire circumstances that brought them together, to here, in this meadow. They made love.

Afterwards, they lay in the grass looking up at the sky, with Dianne resting her head on Fallon's chest. Some starlings darted backwards and forwards in the cloudless blueness. Another bird sung its heart out somewhere off to the left in a hedgerow. This moment was perfect, thought Fallon as he looked down at Dianne who was asleep. He moved slightly and she woke. Dianne gave him a squeeze as if she were trying to take the air from his lungs. Her brown eyes gazed into his icy blue ones. She smiled and lay her head on his chest once more.

"What will you do once the war is over?" She asked.

"Return home, I guess." Replied Fallon. "I hadn't really given it much thought, to be honest." She raised her head once more and looked at him. "What about you?" He asked.

"Try to return to some kind of normality, I suppose." She replied with a tinge of sadness in her voice. "How can I do that after all the things I've seen and done?" The two of them pondered that question for a moment.

Then suddenly, she jumped to her feet, grabbed her blouse and shoes and then ran off across the field leaving Fallon trailing far behind. He managed to catch up with her at the boundary fence. They wandered back to the farmhouse hand in hand, their hands swinging rhythmically. They giggled and looked into each other's eyes, stopping to kiss every so often.

Once back at the barn, Dianne asked Phillippe to take a picture of the two of them for her album. The big Frenchman gladly obliged. Once developed, the picture would show a beautiful dark haired woman standing next to a tall handsome man wearing a British Commandos uniform. The picture would remain hidden until after the war, but the moment would remain in Dianne's heart.

The area commander was a Major-General Hubert Kohl, a veteran of the first war, who was quite content to sit out the war in this peaceful paradise until his pension. He was considered a soft touch by his peers, and he was quite happy letting them believe that. He was a round man, think Mister Potato Head in a German uniform.

Complete with silly moustache and circular spectacles that perched across the bridge of his nose. His rosy cheeks went in line with his cheerful personality, unlike most of his fellow officers, Kohl enjoyed a peaceful and prosperous life making his headquarters the local Vineyard. Wine on tap. Kohl enjoyed hosting extravagant parties for party members and visiting local dignitaries.

But his peaceful existence was about to be broken, when he received a telephone call from Altman, reporting a breach in security. Kohl took some convincing to mobilise the troops but reluctantly, he agreed but made it clear that Altman would be dealing with this and if it turned out to be a wild goose chase, he would pay dearly for it. Altman agreed to take full responsibility. The hunt for the fake Major and his driver was on. A cold smile came across Frettchen's face at the news of the search. He immediately called Wiesel to let him know. The two were beside themselves with excitement. Soon it would be playtime!

The alarm went out and two companies of soldiers were mobilized, one inside the chateau with the other being at the nearby village of St. Michael. Lorry engines burst into life and soldiers climbed on board. A Sd. Kfz 251 half-track started to rumble, a soldier manning the MG-34 machine-gun lurched to and fro as the huge machine lumbered forward. Ten men in the back held on for dear life surrounded by on three sides by heavy armour. Shouting and cursing as locals got in the way.

Meanwhile, Fallon and Dianne, unaware of the coming storm, were walking along the bank of a small stream, laughing and giggling, chasing each other. Conflict played with people's emotions, putting romances on fast forward at times, couples taking full advantage of fleeting moments of calm. Some would just have romances whilst others would walk down the aisle. Families were joined and some would remain glued, but others would be shattered by tragedy. The sun shone down on the couple. During peace time, you would be forgiven for thinking that these two were a couple. Time seemed to speed up.

Before they knew it, it was time for Fallon to return to Britain with the intelligence he had gleaned from his visit to the chateau. The same amount of time that had zoomed for the allies had also sped up for their foes. The searching units had found the burnt out wreck of the Kubelwagen and the find had been reported back to the chateau. Altman had ordered his troops to widen their search area to encompass all outbuildings and farmhouses in the area. No quarter was to be given. The General was still seething for the egg on his face, given to him by Fallon. He felt a laughing stock and wanted his revenge on the fake officer.

The dark shape of the Lysander loomed vulture like as it descended towards the landing field. The same set up as before – six men forming an 'L' shape using lanterns to highlight the area. The machine landed with a bumped and a bounce before settling down. Fallon stood on the edge of the field, his arm around Dianne. He gave her a squeeze and she looked up at him, into his blue eyes and smiled. He bent down and kissed her on the lips.

They savoured the brief contact before releasing each other. Dianne watched from the side lines as Fallon ran towards the Lysander. He climbed up and pulled back the rear canopy, looked back at Dianne, waved, and then climbed aboard, pulling the canopy closed. He signalled to the pilot who pushed the throttle forward and the aircraft moved off.

A shout went up, and Dianne went to one knee, pulling her sten gun off her shoulder. Another shout and then the sound of automatic fire. Dianne looked back over her shoulder just in time to see the dark shape of the lysander taking safely to the sky. She shouted a warning to the half dozen men in the middle of the field, but it fell on deaf ears. They turned to walk back to the thicket just as a burst of machine gun fire tore into the middle of the group.

Two men fell dead whilst the others dived onto their stomachs. Dianne was now in the thicket scanning for the source of the gunfire. Voices shouted from the road that ran alongside the field. German voices. Men could be heard jumping down from the backs of lorries as the half-track gunned its engine as it ploughed through the hedgerow and came into view, the MG-34 chattering as it sprayed tracer bullets in the direction the fleeing bodies in front of it.

Dianne held her sten tightly as she fired a short volley towards the vehicle only to hear the bullets ping off the armour. A French voice shouted, and a small dark shape was thrown towards the halftrack. A grenade exploded inside the vehicle killing all on board. Dianne bolted from cover and ran across the road just as two soldiers came round the corner.

They shouted at her to stop but she kept going. Breathing heavy, she crashed through another hedge row, falling onto her stomach. She slowly got to her knees and looked up, realising she was not alone. A German soldier stood in front of her with his Mauser rifle pointed in her direction. She could see him contemplating whether to shoot her or take her prisoner. Then, for her, all went dark as the butt of a rifle hit her head from behind. The two soldiers each took and arm, dragging the unconscious female towards one of the lorries.

At the chateau, the telephone rang, and Schumann answered. He laid the receiver down on the table and went into the main hall where Altman and Frettchen sat discussing the recent events. Schumann coughed politely and the two men stopped their conversation.

"What is it, Schumann? News of the search?"

"No, Herr General. A telephone call for you."

"Take a message, man! Can't you see I am busy?"

"I am sorry, Sir, but the man on the other end insists he speaks to you." Apologised Schumann.

"Take a number and I will call him back!" Bellowed Altman.

"He said you would fob him off, Sir, and told me to mention one word...."

"Well, spit it out!"

"Skorpion."

The colour drained from Altman's face, and he broke into a cold sweat. Even Frettchen noticed the sudden change.

"Are you alright, Herr General?" Asked the Gestapo officer.

"Er. yes. I am fine. I must, however, excuse myself and take this message." Said Altman getting to his feet, taking a handkerchief from his shirt pocket, and dabbing his forehead as he raced out of the room. He went into his office and picked up the extension. "Yes. Who is this?" He demanded.

"Altman?"

"Yes, who is this?"

"Skorpion."

"I was told you wouldn't be contacting me until the mission was completed."

"Do you still believe the orders you are following are from Berlin, Herr General?"

"Of course. I've just had a conversation with the Fuhrer himself. I would recognise his voice anywhere."

"The conversation was with the Fuhrer, but he thinks you are talking about a totally different mission...."

"But how?"

"Our agents in Berlin swapped the folders before they reached him, and we are monitoring every communications out of the Reichstag."

"Who's 'we'?"

"Why the organisation you have been working for since you were assigned to this mission."

"Who?"

"Setenta Ocho."

"Seventy-Eight? Never heard of you!"

"And you wouldn't have, if you hadn't let a British agent discover what you are really doing at the chateau..." Informed the voice.

"How did you know about that? It has only just happened."

"We have our sources..."

"I am going to inform security of this breach and they will hunt you down!" Altman threatened, panic in his voice.

"This call cannot be traced and how are you going to recognise me? All you have is a name. Don't be foolish, Herr General!" Chastised the voice. "If you were lucky enough to find me, there are others to take my place and what of your family?"

"My family? What do they have to do with this?" Altman asked, looking around his office checking to see if he was still alone.

"We have operatives watching them back in Bavaria, and nothing will happen to them, as long as you continue to follow instructions."

"You bastard!" Yelled Altman.

"Now, now, Herr General. Keep your temper under control and just obey your orders."

"But what about the Fuhrer and my superiors in Berlin?"

"They will continue to be fed information that we will supply them, and as far as they are concerned, you will be accomplishing your mission and be a hero of the Reich."

"But…"

"Setenta Ocho!" The line went dead, leaving Altman standing there like a bride that has just been left at the altar. The office door opened, and Schumann entered.

"Is everything alright, Herr General?"

"What? Err… yes. Fine!" Replied Altman still a little flustered. He walked over and poured himself a stiff drink, downing it in one gulp.

"Bad news, Sir?" Inquired his Aide.

"What? No, just new orders from Berlin. That's all." He fumbled his words before coughing, using this to regain his composure. "Schumann?"

"Sir?"

"I want all the files on my desk relating to Operation Storm."

"But why, Sir?"

"Just do it!" Altman ordered, his frustration boiling over like a pot overheating on the stove. "If anyone asks, I am conducting a review of our procedures."

"As you request, Sir."

"Schumann?"

"Sir?"

"I also want everything on a group called Setenta Ocho."

"Setenta Ocho?" Repeated his Aide.

"Is there an echo in the building? I have given you an order, Hauptman, and I expect it to be carried out!"

"At once, Mein General." Schumann clicked his heels together and saluted, not the Nazi salute but the normal Army one, and then left, closing the door behind him.

Altman poured himself another drink. He used his other hand to steady his shaking hand as he brought it to his lips. He was an army officer.

A veteran of the First World War. He had seen horrors that most men would crack under, and he had held his nerve rising to the rank he presently holds. So why was he shaking now? There was something about the voice on the other end of the line that was menacing.

A voice without substance but with the power to reach out and hold him to ransom, using his family as hostages. This organisation the voice mentioned, Setenta Ocho, had the infrastructure in place to manipulate members within the German government and yet, he had never heard of them. According to the voice, they had operatives everywhere. The thought of this last statement began to make him feel paranoid. Who could he trust? Was Schumann, his trusted aide of over a decade, an agent of Setenta Ocho? And who else?

9 – Skorpion

Fallon's body took a battering in the back of the Lysander on the return trip, funny how he remembered it was more comfortable the outward leg. The twenty mile journey did not take long and before he knew it, the plane was touching down back at its home base. Fallon climbed out and was met by a staff car. Someone was rolling out the red carpet treatment. His ego was deflated when the familiar frame of Smithers got out of the back. The two men saluted and got in the back. No small talk, the two remained silent until they stopped outside OSP headquarters.

"The Colonel is waiting on us in the conference room, K-12." Said Smithers pointing to a door on the right of the main entrance. Fallon followed Smithers, who knocked before entering.

"Ah, Smithers and Fallon. Please, come in." Invited Forrester, more jovial than usual and that worried Fallon. "Good trip?" Forrester asked as the two men sat down.

"Fruitful, I think Sir." Replied Fallon, handing him the roll of film from Phillippe's camera, as well as the label the Frenchman had found on the floor of the truck.

"Excellent. I'll get the boffins on this straight away. Anything else?" Forrester asked, handing off the stuff to Smithers.

"Yes Sir, there is. I would like backgrounds done on a General Altman, and a Gestapo officer named Frettchen."

"Anything else?" Asked Smithers jotting down some notes on a small notepad.

"Any news on my contact, Dianne Gerard? They're seemed to be a bit of a firefight happening as we took off."

"No, K-12. Will you see to it, Smithers."

"I'll give it top priority, Sir." Smithers scuttled away leaving Fallon and Forrester alone.

"Something's bothering you, K-12. What is it?" Asked Forrester putting on his fatherly tone which for a moment, caught the young officer off guard.

"My recon mission was too easy, Sir."

"How so?"

"I mean, the entry to the chateau was simple. The security was laughable even though I was under the constant glare of the guards on the walls, it just seemed too damn easy."

"Sometimes missions go like that, Peter."

Oh Jesus! His boss was using his Christian name! What the hell is going on? Fallon got to his feet, as though making himself taller aided in the thought process. "You said it yourself, Sir, when you sent me on this assignment. There was nothing to see. My French driver was never challenged when he wandered around the trucks, even though there were several soldiers milling about, and that label just happened to be in the truck that he was searching...."

"I'm beginning to see what you mean, K-12. Well, there's nothing we can do about it until we get the photos back, and the chemical mentioned on the label is studied. Go home and catch up on some sleep. A shower too." Fallon smelled under his arm pit. His aroma was a bit on the ripe side. He surrendered to logic and experience, saluted his superior and left.

"What do you mean, you have no data on Setenta Ocho?" Shouted Altman down the telephone. The man on the other end stumbled over his words, trying to explain that he had tried his upmost to glean any information on the secretive organisation he could, but with every turn, he hit either a roadblock of bureaucratic red tape or a door slammed in his face.

"So, what you're trying to tell me is that someone is either protecting this organisation or it doesn't exist?" An affirmative answer on the other end, although sheepishly delivered. "What is your best guess?" Altman waited as the man tried to phrase his response properly, "a cover-up. I see. Danke." He slammed the receiver down and swore.

He was back to the proverbial square one. His personal drawing board, if you like, was getting larger every time he asked questions about this group. The restraints tying his hands were getting tighter and this only infuriated him even more. How high does this go? The Fuhrer himself? Surely not.

The voice on the other end, Skorpion, did say that the group had their tentacles in every level of life from the lowliest soldier to the highest ranking decision makers. Diplomacy was now laughable if their reach extended there too. Was it just the Germans who were infected with this cancer or was their reach Global?

Because of the state of the world due to the conflict, it would be impossible for him to answer his own question. He felt alone. When he took this assignment, his sense of pride overwhelmed him because he thought he was doing it to aid in the war effort, not be some lap dog for some shadowy organisation!

According to Skorpion, the daily reports were still being sent to, and received by, Berlin. So as far as they were concerned, everything was going according to their grand plan. He was still thinking this over when his telephone rang. He picked it up. It was Schumann informing him that they had captured a couple of Maquis.

"What do you want done with them, Herr General?"

"Bring them to the chateau, I want to interrogate them myself."

"But Herr General! What about the standing orders issued by the Fuhrer that all Maquis are to be handed over immediately to the Gestapo?"

"Are you going deaf, Hauptmann Schumann?"

"No Sir."

"Then, carry out my orders."

"At once, Sir."

"Finally, some answers."

Half an hour later, Dianne Gerard and Phillippe were manhandled into the main hall where Altman sat at the end of a long table. It was set out for an evening meal with three place settings, one, which was his, was at the head of the table whilst the other two faced each other at the other end.

"Please sit." Invited Altman. The two Maquis looked suspiciously at Altman and then at each other. Dianne nodded and they took their seats. "Schumann, tell the chef that we are ready."

"But Herr General!" Protested Schumann again.

"Schumann? I am a civilized man and not one of those animals from the Gestapo. Please tell the chef."

"At once." Surrendered Schumann clicking his heels and leaving. Two armed guards stood either side of the doorway, their MP-30s pointed at the two *'guests'*. Altman noticed and tutted loudly before telling them to go away, the lead guard opened his mouth to protest but then thought better of it.

The door behind Altman opened and several men dressed in white jackets entered carrying various trays of food stuffs ranging from a selection of cold meats, steaming boiled and mashed potatoes as well as several types of cooked vegetables.

"Please, help yourselves." Invited Altman reaching over and helping himself to a couple of slices of ham, a large dollop of mash, and some vegetables, including carrots, peas, and corn. "In case you think of trying something stupid..." He warned, bringing up his Luger pistol and placing it beside his plate, "I would strongly recommend you put those thoughts out of your head, sit back, and enjoy the meal. You look as if you're hungry." Realising their current position was hopeless, the two Maquis gave in and reached for the food.

A bottle of wine appeared minutes later, one of the white coated men poured a sample in an empty glass and the General took a sip. "A cheap little vintage but it will suit our purposes." He nodded his approval, and the steward poured the liquid up to the top of the glass. He did the same for the guests before leaving. The two Maquis devoured the food as if they had not eaten in days. It made their host smile with pleasure. Good hospitality could be returned back with information without the need for violence. At least, that is what he hoped.

After the meal and drinks, the three of them retired to the couches as if they were long lost friends. Altman intentionally oozed an air of relaxation and friendship because, in his extensive experience, which was the best atmosphere to get results – true results, rather than the viciousness of the Gestapo method which, eventually, would get the results the interrogator wanted to hear but not necessarily the truth. However, with this type of openness, a cloud hung over the proceedings, the Luger that Altman had close at hand.

Openness was one thing, but trust had to be earned, on both sides. Phillippe looked as though he had fallen for this joviality, he was laughing and joking with the General. Cognac had that effect on him, breaking down walls and loosening his tongue.

Dianne, on the other hand, was more guarded and suspicious. She had seen how the Germans worked close at hand. One minute liberators, the next, worse than their predecessors. She had also heard some of the older members of the village recant horror stories from the first conflict, so her walls were well and truly built up, getting higher by the minute.

She would look around the room every so often checking for escape routes, as well as seeing if anything had changed, like more company that they were too intoxicated to notice the first time around. This, for the moment, had not changed but she still remained on her guard.

Schumann entered and stood in the doorway. He motioned to the General to come over. His superior sighed, got to his feet, excused himself and went over.

"Investigator Frettchen has called again, Mein General." Informed Schumann.

"And? What does our little weasel want now?" Replied Altman angrily.

"A progress report."

Altman looked over at his two '*guests*', one was still acting like a caged animal, whilst the other was almost drunk, both with the alcohol, and the company, in equal measures.

"Soon, Schumann. Soon."

"I am sorry, Sir, but I think Herr Frettchen will want a more definite answer than that."

"Tell the little weasel that I will hand the prisoners over to him when I am done with them! Is that clear?"

"Sir."

"Now, my friends, more cognac?" Asked Altman switching from official mode to charm mode as he re-joined the two on the couches.

10 – LD-27

Fallon lay there in his bath, smoking a cigarette, and exhaling, watching the smoke rings float up to the ceiling and disappear. His body still ached from the plane ride, and he thought, wrongly, that a nice warm soak in a bath would ease the pain. He just lay there enjoying the peace and tranquillity knowing that it would not last long, for once, something that he had gotten right. The doorbell rang. He decided to ignore it and sank under the water.

However, he could still hear it, muffled as it was by the water. He came up for air and cursed his luck. Climbing out, being careful not to slip on the wet surface of his bathroom floor, he wrapped a large towel around his waist and went out into the hallway. He could see a figure silhouetted in the glass of his main door. He unlocked the door and opened the door, just enough to peek out. He cursed again. It was Smithers who smiled back at him.

"Sorry old chap." Smithers apologised pushing his way past, "but the General wants you back at HQ as quick as possible."

"Do I have time to change?" Asked Fallon looking down at the towel, the only thing maintaining his dignity.

"Ah. Oh yes. Very good." Replied Smithers moving into the front room to wait.

Fallon went through to the bedroom, which was to the left of the main door, closing the door for some privacy, emerging ten minutes later in his uniform, shaved and with his hair neatly in place.

"What's happened?" Asked Fallon as the two of them went out the front door, slamming it shut behind them.

"We've got the results back from your little jaunt across the Channel."

"The LD-27?"

"Yes."

They climbed into the waiting staff car and sped off. The barrage balloons floated high above them, remnants from the bombing campaign that had ended only a couple of months previously. It was a change to either walk or drive the streets, without the wail of air raid sirens going off, and the pounding sound the anti-aircraft guns made as they hunted the skies for enemy planes.

The Blitz, as it was called, lasted from 7th September 1940 to 11th May 1941, and was an intense bombing campaign undertaken by the Germans. For eight months, the Luftwaffe (German Airforce) dropped bombs on London and other strategic cities across Britain, nine thousand bombs were dropped, killing one thousand four hundred and thirteen people, whilst injuring three and a half thousand.

It was during this time that the Office of Special Projects had to deal with the sad loss of one of their own – Gregory Cuthbertson, the equipment officer's oldest son, whom he was grooming to take over in the family business once retirement beckoned. Gregory was supervising some testing of new equipment on the outskirts of the capital. It had been decided by the top brass that all such equipment tests should be carried out at various airfields dotted around the country. Their train of thought being that the places were already Ministry of War properties and security came as a package deal. Although, during the tests themselves, security was amped up considerably with Forrester seconding more OSP operatives to bolster the men already on site.

It was on a cold day in March 1941, Gregory had arrived early and was prepping the equipment ahead of the top brasses inspection later that morning. He was in a hangar with three other technicians from the Ministry and he was going over his final checks when an air raid siren stared to wail somewhere on the base. The RAF personnel started to run for the shelters and dugout trenches that littered the sides of the runways. The techs too, took the hint and started to run towards the exit door of the hangar.

One stopped and looked back, he urged Gregory to come with him but being the tech that he is, Gregory waved him off, stating that he would follow along once the finally checks had been completed. For a moment, the other technician thought about forcibly manhandling Cuthbertson to the nearest shelter but when he heard the dull drone of approaching aircraft, his own fight or flight mode kicked in and he sprinted out of the door.

THUMP! THUMP! THUMP! Went the sound of the anti-aircraft guns. Clouds of grey and black smoke peppered the sky as black dots suddenly appeared in the heavens, gradually getting larger as they approached. Heinkel He 111P. Dornier Do 17Z. Messerschmitt Me 110. All accompanied by Messerschmitt Me 109s and Focke Wulf 190 fighters. Pilots on the ground ran to their awaiting aircraft – Hawker Hurricanes and Supermarine Spitfires, ground crews already busying themselves preparing the aircraft for flight. Then came the sound... a high pitch whistle. The German bombers had opened their bomb bays and started to drop their payloads. Across the other side of the runway, two men ran to a machine gun post which was surrounded with sandbags. One of them grabbed the handles of the twin Lewis machine guns and spun around, aiming the weapons at the approaching enemy. The other man stood and pointed out targets to hit.

The Lewis guns opened up. But with an effective range of only eight hundred and eighty yards (eight hundred and five metres), it was like trying to swat a fly with a flimsy piece of paper. Shouts went up. Men screaming. A fuel truck got a direct hit and burst into flames. The fighters on the ground barely managed to get off the ground. Two were strafed by a passing Me109. One burst into flames whilst the other twisted and turned its way along the runway before going nose first into a bomb crater.

POP! POP! POP! Went the bombs as they landed. Ever edging closer and closer to where Gregory was. He found himself ducking a couple of times instinctively before he was finally satisfied his work was done for the moment. He started to run towards the door and then he heard it – the whistle of a bomb. For some unexplainable reason, he stopped and looked up, peering up towards the roof of the hangar as if he could see through it. He did not know what hit him as the whole building exploded outwards as a red and orange fireball engulfed it. No one noticed what happened to Gregory on that day, at that moment. They were all too busy ducking from the onslaught from above. The swarm of enemy planes seemed to crawl across the sky, but they eventually moved on to their next target leaving death and devastation in their wake.

Ambulance bells jingled. People cried and shouted. Someone was shouting instructions. Another noise joined the orchestral sound of doom – the all-clear klaxon. Gerald Cuthbertson was busy in his workshop deep in the bowels of OSP headquarters when he received the news of his son's demise. That sorrowful task was given to his superior, John Forrester, to break it to him. Forrester appeared in the doorway and was greeted by a welcoming smile from Cuthbertson, who was pleasantly surprised to see his superior gracing his section with his presence. The smile soon disappeared when he saw the look on Forrester's face.

"What's happened?" Asked Cuthbertson.

"Can I speak to you in your office, please, Gerald?" Requested Forrester, extending an arm towards the back of the room where Cuthbertson's office was situated. An office? More a table, telephone and a couple of chairs but

Cuthbertson called it his office. Sacrifices had to be made for the greater good. There was a war on, you know. The two men made their way across the floor, watched by the technicians from their individual benches. Some glancing across at each other with worried looks on their faces, whilst others simply shrugged their shoulders. Forrester guided Cuthbertson into the small room and closed the door.

There was the briefest of discussions, at the end of which, Cuthbertson sank to his knees as the enormity of what he had just been told hit him. He crumped to the ground like a heavyweight boxer after receiving a hard body blow to the stomach. Forrester stepped forward, offering a sympathetic hand but Cuthbertson waved it away as he pulled himself upright, tears streaming down his face. Another conversation. A shake of the head from Cuthbertson and the door to the office opened, Forrester walked slowly out and across the floor towards the exit.

All eyes moved to the office door. Cuthbertson stood behind his desk, propped up by his hand, looking straight ahead. He coughed. Used the back of his sleeve to wipe away the tears and then walked slowly to the doorway.

"Right!" He said. "What is everyone staring at?" He choked back the tears. It was clear to all those in the room that he was struggling to maintain his composure. "Come on, back to work!" He ordered. "There's a war on....you know." He paused before uttering the last couple of words as his legs gave out once more. His arm shot out and grabbed the side of the doorframe, stopping himself from collapsing onto the ground.

He looked around the room with tear filled eyes, his bottom lip quivering, nodded his head a couple of times and then went back into the office, closing the door behind him.

He walked slowly around to the other side of the table and stared down at the black telephone in front of him. He sighed, shook his head and then picked up the receiver. A conversation was had. The hardest one an individual could have. The one where you have to tell your spouse that one of your children has died. Tears flowed once more. Legs buckled and Cuthbertson flopped down into a nearby chair.

But that was almost a year ago and time waits for no man. Cuthbertson took a couple of days off to bury his son in the cemetery close to where he stayed. It was a simple affair. No bells and whistles. Just immediate family and some colleagues from work and then it was back to devising devilish ways to defeat the enemy. When he returned, Cuthbertson was a different man. More driven. He had decided to channel his grief. Burying himself into his work. He would get his revenge on those that had taken his son from him and the best way for him to do that was to work and work damn hard.

The streets carried the scars of bombed out buildings and huge piles of rubble. It took a skilled driver to navigate his way around the city and at speed. After ten minutes of dodging and weaving, their staff car came around the top of the street where OSP headquarters was. The car stopped right outside the entrance and the two officers climbed out. A burly Sergeant stepped forward and asked for their identification papers. Fallon gave a puzzled looked at Smithers.

"New security measures, old boy. The Colonel instigated them due to the rash of leaks the other agencies have been having recently. Fifth column and all that." Explained Smithers as the two men showed the required documents before heading inside. Instead of heading upstairs like they would do normally, Smithers veered to the right and knocked on one of two glass panelled doors before entering. Fallon and Smithers were greeted by Forrester, sitting in the front of a line of three chairs along with an admiral, and Cuthbertson was standing at the back of the room guarding a projector. Both men stood to attention.

"Enough of that rubbish, gentlemen, and sit down." Dismissed Forrester, "Admiral Harrison Lusk. Fallon and Smithers." Forrester did the introductions. "Now down to why I've called you here. What you're about to see was smuggled out of occupied France by one of our resistance contacts. Sad to say, the poor fellow was shot and killed shortly after passing this on to us." He signalled to Cuthbertson who switched off the lights and then started the projector. It whirred into life. After a few short flashes of a countdown, the main feature began. It showed a man sitting in a chair. The commentary, in German, told the officers that the man was a local resistance leader that had been apprehended during a routine sweep of the area.

A man came into shot, wearing the same protective rubberised suit and gas mask that Fallon had seen at the chateau, carrying a canister with LD-27 written on the side of it. The man placed the canister in front of the man who, the assembled audience could now see had been restrained around the waist and legs by ropes. The narrator went on to explain that the suited man would now pull the pin on the canister, like you would if you were about to throw a grenade.

With the pin pulled, the man made a hasty exit leaving the camera focused on the captive. Instantly, the man in the chair started to tremble, then started to violently convulse. Within a few minutes, the man in the chair stopped moving and was clearly deceased. The audience, to a man, felt both sick and repulsed by what they had just witnessed. Forrester waved at Cuthbertson to stop the projector. He stood up just as the lights went back on and turned to the room. He nodded towards Cuthbertson who stepped forward.

"LD-27. Similar to the more infamous Sarin. It attacks the central nervous system causing paralysis and peripherally medicated respiratory arrest, leading, as we have just witnessed, to death. It is clear, colourless, tasteless, and has no smell in its purest form. Like Sarin, the Nazis developed it originally as a pesticide in the late thirties…"

"How deadly is this stuff?" Asked Lusk.

"It is lethal to fifty percent of those exposed to doses of one hundred to five hundred milligrams across the skin, or fifty to one hundred milligrams by inhalation in an average person weighing seventy kilograms." Said the equipment officer clinically, as if he were reading the ingredients off of a tin.

"Jesus Christ!" Said Lusk.

"How can it be delivered?" Asked Smithers.

"One way has just been demonstrated on the film...." Replied Cuthbertson, "but I think, according to our sources, whatever is going on at that chateau, they plan to deliver it on a much larger scale than simply placing it on the ground and running away to safety."

"Agreed." Added Forrester, "and that's the reason I have asked admiral Lusk to join us today. The Admiral is in charge of the submarine fleet that protect the home waters. I have asked him if we could borrow one of his boats to ferry a commando raiding party to the chateau to gather intelligence on what they're doing and stop it if needs be." That explains why Fallon and Smithers were asked to attend as well. "Smithers?"

"Sir."

"I want you to gather all the Intel we have, and coordinate with admiral Lusk, I want you to formulate a plan of attack. Fallon?"

"Sir."

"It's your job to lead the search and destroy mission."

"Understood, Sir."

"We have to stop these bastards before they can put whatever they have planned into operation!" He surveyed the room looking for any sign of doubt or questions. Nothing. "Dismissed."

Two days later, Fallon received a telephone call from Smithers requesting his presence back at headquarters. Once there, Fallon returned to the conference room. It looked remarkably different to the last time he was there.

Gone were the projector and the three lines of chairs, in their place was a large table, with five chairs spaced around the perimeter, a large map pinned to the wall behind the table and a smaller table with a choice of either water or tea to drink, a large metal urn was hissing away in the corner, ready to spew out piping hot water on demand. To him, it looked like it was going to be a long session.

He was first to arrive and took his chance to survey the map on the wall. It was a general map of France but had been blown up to allow for more detailed examination. Suddenly, the door opened and in walked Forrester, Lusk, and Smithers, as usual taking up the rear. Forrester asked them all to take a seat as he dropped a sizable pile of folders onto the main desk.

"Gentlemen," he began, placing his hands on the table and leaning on them, "the storm is really hitting the fan with this one." He opened the top file and passed it to Smithers who distributed the contents. "According to our sources deep within the Nazi hierarchy, Hitler knows nothing about what is really going on at the chateau. He thinks they are carrying out research into a new explosive that could end the war within six weeks, if perfected."

"So, he has no idea about LD-27?" Asked Lusk.

"According to our sources, he is firmly against using any chemical warfare against the Allies. Some of his top brass wanted to use Sarin, and he has refused point blank. Our leading analysts think his aversion to this has something to do with some traumatic incident during the Great War."

"I see."

"But, Sir," butted in Fallon, "can we now address the elephant in the room? Who is behind the chateau if it's not the Nazis?"

"Good question. Smithers, can you answer that please." Said Forrester looking over at his aide.

"Yes Sir. According to one of our operatives in Madrid, Spain, there is rumbles that a new group behind the goings on at the chateau. May I, Sir?" He asked reaching for the next file. Forrester stood back, out of the way, allowing him past. He took the top file, opened it and like the previous one, handed out the contents individually. "The group is called Setenta Ocho, that's seventy-eight in Spanish. The actual origins of the group are pretty sketchy, but they are believed to have started in Madrid around the beginning of this century..."

"Set up by whom?" Asked Forrester.

"No definite names, Sir, but it is believed a group of industrialists were behind it. They were unhappy with the financial markets and decided to do something about it. Since then, it would appear that they have their interests in everything from intelligence gathering to politics to banking and that's just their legitimate dealings. According to intel, they also have their tentacles in organised crime from prostitution, gambling, arms dealing and even the sordid world of drug dealing..."

"Interesting use of the word 'tentacles,' Smithers." Commented Forrester.

"Thank you, Sir. I like to refer to them as an octopus because their dealings are so diverse that you would need several arms to juggle them."

"How are members of this organisation recognised?" Asked Lusk.

"In public, you wouldn't be able to tell because they stay in the shadows. However, when they meet as a group, the members are rumoured to wear a large ring on their left ring finger. It is gold with a black stone, with gold numbers on the stone."

"Excuse me for raising this obvious point," said Lusk, "but all I have heard is rumour this and rumour that. If you ask me, it's all speculation. I would need solid proof before we could take this to the Minister for approval."

"What about the chateau? The movie we saw here but a few hours ago. Is that proof enough to at least investigated what the hell is going on?" Pleaded Fallon who, up until then, had remained silent allowing himself to absorb the two-ing and froing as if he were spectating at a tennis match.

"ENOUGH!" Yelled Forrester thumping his hand down on the table. "Gentlemen, this is getting us nowhere. Smithers, can you please continue with your briefing."

"Of course, Sir, and thank you. Gentlemen, the mission will proceed like this. A commando raiding party will be depart from a submarine one mile off the coast and paddle in. They will then hike to the chateau and gather more intel before assaulting the target. The assault team, led by Lieutenant Fallon. He is familiar with the area and has the necessary military training. The main mission is to stop production of LD-27 and destroy any stockpiles the Germans have.

A side mission would be to gain as much intel as possible about both the LD-27 and Setenta Ocho. Any personnel they can capture would be a bonus, adding to the said intel. The final part of the mission would be for them to be extracted by submarine and brought back safely to base."

"Thank you, Smithers. Questions?" Asked Forrester looking around the room. Silence. "Gentlemen, I now have to take this to the PM for his approval. I surely don't have to remind you that this briefing is covered by a D-notice, meaning that it is not to be discussed with anyone outside this room." Everyone nodded their understanding of the situation.

11 – HMS Spectre

HMS Spectre was an S-class submarine of his Majesty's Royal Navy. A member of the silent service. She was two hundred and seventeen feet long and twenty-three feet nine inches wide, with a top speed of twenty-eight kilometres per hour (seventeen miles per hour) on the surface and nineteen kilometres per hour (twelve miles per hour) submerged.

Six bow torpedo tubes and one in the stern measuring twenty-one inches (five hundred and thirty-three millimetres). She, like any lady, could defend herself when cornered. Three fifty calibre Browning machine guns for offence, these were removed whilst the boat was submerged, and one three inch (seventy six millimetre) deck gun and one point eight inch (twenty millimetre) anti-aircraft gun for defence.

She was currently undergoing some minor repairs after her last sortie into the cold and forbidding North Sea. Her usual mission was patrolling the home waters looking out for enemy targets and dispatching them to the bottom, or Davey Jones' locker to use a nautical reference. The crew of forty-three were like a family. They had joined the boat shortly after she had been commissioned and had stayed together through thick and thin. Being a submariner was not a glamourous life. Stuck together for months on end, in cramped, smelly conditions can either bond men together or serve to traumatise them.

Whilst on shore, it was strict Navy regulations when it came to behaviour and attire. Uniforms must be worn, and etiquette followed at all times. Saluting and 'yes Sir' were mandatory. On patrol, however, this went out of the window. The only person who was treated with the proper Naval decorum was the Captain. Saluting was shelved but 'Sir' remained.

Although the commander of the boat was referred to as Captain, in reality, his rank was often a Lieutenant. Since being commissioned in 1935, Spectre had had three commanding officers – Lieutenants David Smith, Kieran Spalding and her present commander, Geordie Harrow.

One of the things that made the Spectre stand out from the crowd was the fact that, on her conning tower, was painted a smiling ghost riding a torpedo. The Admiralty usually frowned on people defacing government property but for some reason, when it came to the '*silent service*' nothing was done about it. Some said that it was a morale boosting exercise, and others, that it added character to the boat. Whichever side of the fence you took to sit on, seeing this caricature on the side of the machine that was attacking you certainly left its mark both physically and mentally.

In fact, it was later found out by an historian, several years later, who, whilst researching the submarine war during this conflict, that the submarine with the phantom on the conning tower was mentioned several times in Kriegsmarine (German Navy) communiques between Admiral Donitz and Berlin, especially when it came to the sinking of the supply shipping in and around Area 'X.' But that was all in the future. For the moment, most of the crew were ashore enjoying some down time whilst their boat was being repaired.

Lieutenant Geordie Harrow, on the other hand, was in the back of a staff car on his way to the Capital after being summoned by Admiral Harrison Lusk. As per usual, when a junior officer is summoned by a superior, it is natural for him to go through his mind wondering what he had done wrong. Mistakes made during their deployment both tactical and the more mundane. He had not had time to even get properly changed before being whisked away or even shave. The young officer looked a disgraceful sight as he climbed out of the back of the staff car and made his way up the stairs.

The sentries had to take a double take before saluting this person, who looked more like a hobo that had lost his way, than a naval officer. He nervously returned their salute before entering the imposing building. He made his way up the large spiral staircase to the second level and followed the signs that pointed him in the direction of Lusk's office. He knocked on the door and entered. To his surprise, he found himself in an outer office and not the main one, like he had expected. A Wren sat behind a desk typing away. She paused as he entered.

"Lieutenant Harrow?" She asked.

"Yes."

"One moment." She picked up a telephone, "Lieutenant Harrow to see you, Sir. Very well." She replaced the receiver. "You can go in now, Lieutenant." She said before returning to her typing. Harrow knocked and then went in.

Lusk sat behind his desk as Harrow entered. He looked quite an imposing figure sitting there. The light bouncing off his bald head, which shone like a beacon of hair loss. Lusk was a heavy-set man, who's stomach protruded under his tunic, a handy place to place one's tray whilst eating. He stood up as the young officer approached and saluted, Lusk saluted and then sat down. "Harrow, take a seat."

"Sir." The Lieutenant removed his cap and sat down. The nerves were bubbling inside him like lava in a volcano.

"Relax." Said Lusk reading over a file before closing it. "How was your last trip?"

"Bagged two freighters and would've had a third, if we hadn't run up against that escort cruiser, Sir."

"Yes. I've read your after action report. You were lucky to get away."

"Lucky, Sir? I don't know what you mean."

"Your boat got pretty banged up under that depth charge barrage. I'd say you were lucky; wouldn't you agree?"

"If that's your assessment Sir, then I guess I have to agree with you." A tone of defiance in the young officer's voice made Lusk raise a quizzical eyebrow.

"Really Lieutenant? I guess from your tone, you disagree?"

"Permission to speak frankly, Sir?"

Lusk nodded.

"Damn it, Sir! I could have gotten the cruiser, and the freighter, but caution intervened."

"Caution? More like common sense."

"If you say so Sir." Replied Harrow deflated.

"The privilege of rank, Lieutenant."

"If you don't mind me asking Sir, am I here to get reprimanded or what?" Asked Harrow trying to force the issue.

"I need you for a special operation," began Lusk putting his hands together and placing them on the table with his fingers pointing upwards. He rested one of his chins on them before continuing, "I have taken Spectre out of service…"

"But Sir, that's not fair!" Protested the young officer.

"War isn't fair, Lieutenant." Reminded Lusk, "I have taken Spectre out of service to assist on a little jaunt the intelligence chappies want a hand with. You will ferry a group of commandos to a map reference mentioned in your orders, submerge, and wait for their return. Clear?"

"Sir." Harrow said reluctantly taking the manila envelope from Lusk.

"This mission is top secret and cannot be discussed with anyone except your first officer. As far as the rest of your crew is concerned, you are dropping the soldiers off and returning to base."

"Understood."

"And Harrow."

"Sir?"

"I cannot stress how important the success of this mission is."

"Understood Sir." Harrow saluted and left. Lusk looked down at his desk at the folder Forrester had given him several hours earlier. A couple of photographs that had been lifted from the home movie they had watched, stared back at him. It showed the man tied to the chair. One had him just sitting there like he was watching something off camera. The second showed him in full convulsion. It made the hardened naval officer shiver and feel queasy.

"How could one human being do this to another?" He said out loud, more to try and ease his conscience than to get an answer he was alone in the room. All they needed now was the clearance to go ahead with the mission. They had the transport, HMS Spectre, and now needed the blunt instrument, Fallon, and his commandos.

12 – The Demonstration

The following day, at the chateau, Altman ordered Schumann to bring his guests up from the basement where they had spent the night locked away in one of the less comfortable rooms. Unwashed and now starving, Dianne and Phillippe were brought before him. Altman sat at the large dining table tucking into a hearty breakfast of eggs, bacon and toast washed down by strong coffee. The aroma of the coffee could be smelt out in the anteroom as the guards bundled them through the door.

Phillippe groaned. He was nursing the mother of all hangovers after the frivolity of the night before. Now, began the second phase of Altman's interrogation. Phase one was the carrot, politeness, and frivolity, now came the stick, shouting and if necessary, violence. He hoped that the last part would not be necessary as it made him feel like he had descended down to the level of the Gestapo, and he despised them.

Dianne was put down on a chair whilst the fragile Phillippe was forced to remain standing. A guard covered Dianne with his MP-40 as Altman began his questioning.

"What was the name of the officer you drove to the chateau?"

"Officer, what officer? I am but a humble farmer." Said Phillippe.

"You have been identified as the man dressed as a Corporal, who drove this mysterious officer here. Now I want his NAME!" Altman shouted the last word making Phillippe groan and grab his head.

"Please, what is it with the shouting?" Complained the Frenchman. "I don't know what or who you are talking about, Monsieur." Altman struck him across the face with the back of his hand.

"You lie!" He screamed. "What was his name?" Phillippe regained his posture and shook his head defiantly. Again, a slap. Again, the shake of the head. Altman changed target and punched the Frenchman in the stomach, momentarily knocking the wind out of him causing him to double over. Grabbing his hair, Altman went in close, spitting every word in Phillippe's face. "What was his name?" Phillippe responded with a stupid smile before speaking.

"I think you could do with a breath mint, Herr General. Someone has very bad morning breath. Phew!" He said wafting his hand up at his nose to exaggerate his point and at a feeble attempt at mockery. It failed on that count but managed to rile the General's temper.

"You may not want to talk but perhaps your female friend will." He looked over at Dianne who shook her head. "Ah, but you will my dear. Take the man to the room." Phillippe's smile disappeared to be replaced by a look of sheer terror. He had heard stories of a room in the chateau that when you enter, you never come out, alive anyway.

Two guards stepped forward and grabbed Phillippe under the armpits and dragged him off, down some stairs in the hallway, into the basement, along a dimly lit corridor to a room at the end of it, accessed through a heavy metal door, with a wheel to open and close it, situated about stomach height.

Another guard was already turning the wheel as the threesome approached. The door opened like the jaws of some behemoth ready to swallow its prey. Phillippe was manhandled into a small square room with a light bulb swinging from a flex in the centre of the ceiling, and a large window facing a single wooden chair with leather restraints bolted to it.

Phillippe was tied to the chair. Straps around his wrists, his chest and both ankles. Finally, they restrained his head with a strap that went across his forehead, thus fixing his gaze towards the window. The guards left and a buzzing sound could then be heard as someone picked up a microphone. It was Altman's voice, Phillippe heard next.

"This is your last chance. Tell me who the officer was." Demanded Altman, almost pleading with Phillippe, who just gave his trademark stupid grin and tried to shake his head the best he could, considering the head restraint. "Very well. Titus, it is over to you."

A man appeared in the doorway, wearing a yellow rubberized suit that covered his whole body and a gas mask over his face, carrying a small canister with the letters and numbers LD-27 printed in bold type on its side. He placed the canister in front of the Frenchman. The man bent down and pulled the small ring pull like tab on the top of the canister before making a quick exit. The heavy metal door closed with a heavy clunk as the wheel was turned, it sounded like an angry wasp according to Phillippe, or was that the LD-27 starting to take effect.

From behind the safety of the glass, Dianne watched the effects of the gas with horror, tears streaming down her face. Three times she grabbed Altman's tunic, begging him to stop, but he just looked at her and shook his head, stating that it was too late. It was over within seconds. Altman turned to Dianne, as a soldier flicked a switch turning off the light in the room opposite.

"Now, tell me the name of the officer that came to the chateau, or you will meet a similar fate to your brave but stupid friend next door." He threatened.

"His name was Louis." Whispered Dianne through the tears.

"Very good, my dear. Louis what?"

"Serpens."

Altman took out a notebook from his left tunic pocket and a pencil, noted down the name and then motioned for the guard to take Dianne away. He waited until he was alone, before walking over to a telephone hanging on the wall and dialled for an internal number. It buzzed twice before Schumann answered.

"Schumann, get me everything the Feldjager have on a Louis Serpens."

"Why the military police, Mein General?"

"Because I have a feeling, I've heard this name before, and it's something to do with a military operation in the past, but I can't place my finger on it."

"At once, Mein General." Schumann clicked his heels together, turned and left the room.

Altman put the telephone down and went back upstairs where he was greeted by an exasperated Frettchen.

"Ah, Frettchen. I thought I smelt your repugnant odour as I came upstairs. For a moment, I thought I had stood in something unpleasant. It would appear, by your presence, I was mistaken." Altman walked across to his drinks table, and helped himself to a drink, not bothering to offer the Gestapo officer one, he sat down on the couch facing him. "What can I do for you?" He asked taking a sip, as if he was trying to rinse a bad taste from his mouth.

"My intelligence officers tell me that you have two Maquis prisoners here, in the chateau."

"Gestapo and intelligence. Well, there's two words I didn't think I would hear uttered in the same sentence."

"I warn you, General!"

"You warn me!" Bellowed Altman jumping to his feet, "may I remind you that any security matters pertaining to this district still fall under my purview, and you are only here as a courtesy!"

"And my I remind you, Herr General, that if you have these saboteurs, then they fall under my jurisdiction, as per the Fuhrer's mandate, or need I remind you of the fact?"

"Nein! Nein! You don't have to remind me." Altman took another drink, "anyhow, I don't have two Maquis…"

"But my intelligence."

"I have one. The other died under interrogation." Admitted Altman emptying his glass and getting up for a refill.

"Under the…" Began Frettchen.

"Under the Fuhrer's mandate, there must be an officer from the Gestapo present. BLAH! BLAH! BLAH!" Said Altman waving his hand away. "I am familiar with all your bureaucratic nonsense. Now leave me Frettchen. I have an enormous headache and you are beginning to bore me."

"You haven't heard the last of this General!" Shouted Frettchen storming out, like a schoolboy who has had his favourite toy taken off of him, as a punishment for bad behaviour.

"Yeah…yeah. Whatever!" Replied Altman taking a large gulp from his glass as he watched the leather coated weasel storm out to his car, through a window, and taking several goes to open the door, which Altman could only assume, would stoke his fury, got in, yelled at his driver, before driving off. It was a small insignificant victory on his part, but Altman knew that the weasel would go above his head and get his way in the long run. Schumann walked in.

"Excuse me, Mein General." He handed Altman an official looking envelope. The senior officer looked at him with a puzzled look on his face. Schumann raised his hands signifying that he had nothing to do with it.

"It just arrived by special messenger with the strict instructions for your eyes only, Sir." He turned and walked away. Altman was intrigued. He walked back to his desk and picked up a dagger shaped letter opener, slipped the blade tip into one end and with one fluid movement, opened the envelope.

He tipped the contents on the table and then looked down at them. Two things stared back at him – a folded letter and a large gold ring. He cautiously used the tip of the letter opener to reposition the ring so that he could see the insignia more clearly. He was expecting something like his regimental crest or academy shield. Instead, there was just two numbers – seven and eight. He cursed under his breath before unfolding the enclosed letter.

'*Dear Altman.*

I trust this letter finds you in good health. Please find enclosed a little gift from us to signify your membership of Setenta Ocho, our exclusive little club with immense benefits to its members worldwide. But our board of directors have directed me to inform you that to become a fully-fledged member, you must first complete the mission you have started at the chateau. Within the next few days, you will receive further instructions about this.

Setenta Ocho!
Skorpion.'

Altman stared at the document in front of him, as if he were trying to burn a hole in it. He felt like a rat caught in a trap with nowhere to turn and no one to ask for help, or as the American Western movies were prone to say, 'the calvary would ride in to save the day at the last moment.' He reached into his tunic pocket and took out a box of matches, pushed the slider at one end to reveal the heads of several matches, took one, and rasped the head of it against the sandpaper strip on the long side of the box, igniting it. He held the match to one end of the letter until the flame from it began to play with the flammable paper, catching it, and starting a satisfying flame. He tossed the letter into his ashtray and stood there watching the evidence burn to a crisp.

Next, he picked up the ring, opened the right hand top drawer of his desk and threw it in like you would with a broken toy into a bin. The drawer thudding closed was also strangely enjoyable. Altman took a breath and reviewed his current situation in his head, worried that someone would overhear it he spoke aloud. No one but himself and this '*Skorpion*' knows of his forced membership of this group Seventy-Eight. Tick.

As far as his aide, Schumann, was concerned, it was a progress report he had handed him. Tick. He sat back in his chair, which creaked under the pressure of his excessive weight and a smile started to form on his face. A contented smile like the cat that had got to the saucer of cream first. In his head, he was sticking it to Setenta Ocho and all its minions. It felt good.

13 – Taken

The next morning, as Skorpion had promised, another envelope was handed to Altman by Schumann. It contained orders to ship all of the viable canisters of LD-27 by ship to a place called Peenemunde. He had to go across to his large map behind his desk and search for the place. He eventually found it on the Baltic Sea coast of Germany. He had never been there himself, but he had heard rumours that this was where the Reich were developing some kind of wonder weapon.

Some people, allegedly in the know, even went as far as saying that it was a rocket capable of bringing down massive destruction upon the enemy. Berlin's hope was then for some of the Allied Nations to want peace. This new weapon had a name – Vergeltunswaffe 2 or Retaliation Weapon 2.

The Allies would come to call it simply the V-2. The V-2 was the world's first long-range guided ballistic missile. Altman remembered once, during a visit to Berlin, being briefed on the prospect of such a weapon. The briefing was conducted by a young scientist called Wernher von Braun. From a failed rocket test led by his mentor Rudolph Nabel, in the Summer of 1932, at the rocket research facility of Kummersdorf, twenty miles South of Berlin, Von Braun had become the darling of the German Army. On the day of the briefing, more than five years later, Altman remembered how impressed he was of the enthusiasm of this white coated individual, but thought his ideas were mere pipe dreams. According to latest intelligence, it would appear he had been wrong.

He placed the letter on his desk and relayed the instructions contained in it to Schumann, who noted down the '*bullet*' points so that he would not get them wrong. Schumann nodded every so often, signalling to his superior that he was keeping up and understanding the instructions given. The briefing ended with the obligatory kick of the heels and 'Heil Hitler' salute but after doing it, Schumann also did the normal salute, remembering how Altman hated the first one with a vengeance.

Altman stood, once again, alone in his office. He was glad of this posting and the subterfuge of maintaining the frontage of being a retreat for monks. If this were anywhere else in the Reich, there would be massive red flags with black swastikas hanging from every conceivable place.

There would be similar flags billowing in the wind from the front of the building too, underlining their dominance and, in his guarded opinion, arrogance. Schumann gathered the necessary logistical data and relayed them to Altman over the next few days. Plans were planned and routes were mapped. Altman's inner circle were brought in to consult.

They consisted of a couple of Majors, a Captain and several of the scientists, including Titus, who it had been decided quite early on in the planning, would accompany the canisters to their final destination to supervise the loading and unloading like a father watching over his infants. To say Titus was not happy about this was an understatement but, in accordance with the instructions, Altman just said one phrase and almost immediately, Titus' persona seemed to change before his eyes.

"Setenta Ocho."

Altman was not sure whether the look on Titus' face was fear, compliance, or a mixture of but after that, he became putty in Altman's hands. It was as if Altman had waved a magic wand and changed Titus there and then. It took four trucks to ferry the canisters to the nearest port, some twenty kilometres away where the cargo vessel '*Extremum Fato*' was waiting. Strangely, the crew never acknowledged Altman, or his rank and he did not recognise their uniforms either.

They certainly were not either Wehrmacht, Kriegsmarine, or Luftwaffe personnel. Every single one of them, including the Captain, wore plain black coveralls. No saluting, just industriously unloading the canisters from the lorries and putting them into the hold of the vessel, under the watchful supervision of Titus, of course. Once loaded, the Captain came over and thrust a clipboard into Altman's hands.

"What is this for?" He asked.

"Procedure." Came the one word reply.

"Who's?"

"The leader."

"Ah, the Fuhrer." Said Altman mistakenly, putting pen to paper, and signing his name.

"Who?" Asked the Captain blankly and then he smiled a toothless smile, as he snatched the board from Altman before he could react. The Captain waddled up the gangplank and said something to a couple of deckhands, who then pulled the plank up onto the deck. He started to climb the metal stairs, which led to the bridge but paused halfway and looked down towards Altman. He grinned again and gave him the laziest salute you have ever had the displeasure to witness, before finishing his climb to the summit of his power.

Grabbing a battered and stained megaphone, he put it to his mouth and ordered his crew to castaway the lines, both bow and stern. The horn blew a long depressing tone before smoke started to come from the single funnel just behind the bridge. At the back of the ship, the water started to look as if it was beginning to boil as the vessels propellors started to turn and the ship started to move. From the bridge, the Captain waved. If his movements had been any more exaggerated, Altman was convinced the man would start to fly. A black flag was unfurled on the stern with a red seventy-eight emblazoned in the centre field.

Altman was convinced he heard the Captain laugh even harder, more guttural than the last, like a prankster pulling the largest trick ever over an unsuspecting victim.

As the ship sailed out of port, Altman was puzzled why none of the regular patrolling E-Boats had challenged the departure. Nor were there any loud hails from the harbour master. Just how much influence did this Seventy-Eight group actually have, he wondered as he walked back to his car.

He climbed in the rear, a man with mixed emotions. On one hand, he was glad to get rid of the canisters and on the other, he felt betrayed by his superiors who had failed to keep him in the loop regarding who he was working for, but then a realisation struck him like someone hitting him square in the face with a sledgehammer. What if they did not even know about what was happening? Berlin was certainly being kept in the dark by forces unknown. Correction, by Setenta Ocho.

It was dusk by the time Altman returned to the chateau. The light was getting softer, and the shadows were getting longer as he climbed out of the car. He stretched and yawned. The day was at an end, and he could do with a drink. He slowly climbed the stairs and was greeted by Schumann. The look on his Aide's face made his superior stop.

"What is it, Hauptmann?"

"Herr Frettchen has been, Sir." Schumann said sheepishly. "There was nothing I could do, Mein General."

"Stop wailing like an old woman and tell me what happened." Ordered Altman entering the entrance hall and beginning to unbutton his jacket. His hat was tossed on a nearby chair.

"He, Herr Frettchen, was here just after you left with the convoy…"

"And? Spit it out man!"

"He had an order from the local commandant…"

"Kohl?"

"Yes, Mein General."

"That fat good for nothing!"

"Anyway," Schumann continued, "the Gestapo now have…"

"THE WOMAN!" Altman realised, rushing down the stairs to the basement. He almost ran along the long corridor to her cell and found the door ajar. Schumann eventually caught up, wheezing, and sweating profusely. "You idiot, Schumann!" Yelled Altman.

"But Mein General, he had the correct papers." Whined the Aide like a balloon with its air slowly escaping, "what could I do? Disobey a direct order? They would have shipped me off to the Russian front." Schumann whimpered.

"That's where we'll both be going if we're not careful." Altman pointed out pushing his way past and heading back up the corridor. He went into his office and grabbed the telephone.

"Get me a line to the airfield, immediately." He had just replaced the receiver when the telephone rang. He picked it up. It was the commandant at the local airstrip. Airfield would be too grandiose, for it as it was a field with some tents, and a couple of Messerschmitt 109s and a battered Fokker Wulf Condor reconnaissance aircraft.

"I want that rust bucket of a Condor in the air within the hour. You are looking for a freighter called '*Extremum Fato.*' I want you to track it and tell me where it makes landfall…I don't give a damn that your pilots have been assigned to attack an Allied convoy… This takes priority unless you want to spend your time chipping ice off the wings of your Fokker Wulf 190 on the Russian Front!" He slammed the telephone down.

"Mein General."

"What?" Altman yelled. It was Schumann, recovered from his signs of weakness, he approached his superior with a piece of paper. "What's this, more bad news?"

"The information on Louis Serpens, you requested a few days ago. My apologises for the delay. The intelligence section had to delve deep into the archives."

"Danke." Altman thanked him and took the report. He went to his desk and Schumann walked over to the drinks table, poured out a generous amount of cognac into a glass and placed it next to his superior, Altman nodded his gratitude. Schumann gave a nervous smile and turned to leave. "Hauptman Schumann?" Altman called after him.

"Sir?"

"I am sorry for how I have treated you, my friend."

"I understand, Mein General. You have had a lot on your mind the past few days."

"Danke, my friend." Altman smiled, relieved he had been forgiven. Schumann gave a stiff nod, clicked his heels together and left. He reached for his alcohol as he began to read.

'*Louis Serpens. Underworld assassin for hire. Born in Paris in 1885…*' That first line almost made him choke on his drink. How could that be? That would make Serpens fifty-seven years old. The young man he saw in that fake officer's uniform could not have been more than twenty. Twenty-two on the outside.

'*When Serpens was hired by Alexandre Falcone, which raised a red flag with the security services, in the 1920s to kill an agent of the Office of Special Projects called Jonathan Fallon. Fallon had travelled to Falcone's Island disguised as Serpens in an attempt to rescue his wife and young son, who had been kidnapped by Falcone's son, Lukas, after a minor disagreement in a public house near the Fallons home.*'

Altman stopped reading and took another long slow sip of his cognac, allowing both the drink and the information to seep into his consciousness.

"So, Serpens is an alias used by the Office of Special Projects." He finally said out aloud, piecing together the jigsaw. "So that means, it was an agent of the OSP in my office sampling my finest cognac…" He took another sip and raised the glass, toasting the brass neck this young man had, for entering a secure area the way he did and escaping, without even firing a single shot. If it had not been for the weasel's suspicions, Altman would have been none the wiser.

He smiled and finished off his drink. "I am done with it all now!" He proclaimed putting the report into a paper folder, closing it, and tossing the folder into his out tray. "LD-27 is someone else's problem now and so is that weirdo, Titus!" He raised his glass again to toast to his good fortune and then realised his glass was empty. He let out a booze fuelled laugh before getting to his feet, leaving the office, and staggering up the stairs to his room and bed. It had been a long difficult day and tomorrow, was looking promising.

14 – Departure

Lieutenant Geordie Harrow pulled the collar of his great coat up around his neck as the rain began to come down. The wind had picked up too as he approached the main gate of the submarine base where HMS Spectre was birthed. He showed his identification to one of the sentries, who quickly darted back into the warmth of this sentry box, leaving Harrow to duck under the barrier pole and continue on, battling the wind and the rain, along the quayside until the unmistakable shape of Spectre's conning tower rose up out of the water like the head and neck of some mythical sea monster.

The officer of the watch, a young seaman wrapped up to the nines against the elements, flashed a torch at his credentials, and saluted him as he walked down the gangway and onto the deck of his boat. He found one of the hatches open, climbed hurriedly down the ladder into the belly of the beast and into the warmth and shelter from the outside.

"Good evening, Sir." Welcomed the coxswain, Leslie Warwick. "Nasty outside tonight, isn't it?" He handed Harrow a mug of piping hot tea that the young officer cupped in both hands, allowing the heat from the mug to thaw out his hands.

"Thanks."

"No problem, Sir. Mister MacLeod is forward and would like a word when you have a moment."

"Thank you." Acknowledged Harrow as he went forward, ducking as he went through the hatch. He found his first officer leaning over a map he had laid out on a table. A mixture of concern and concentration on his bearded face. Jessie MacLeod looked up as Harrow approached. "You wanted to see me?" Asked Harrow.

"Aye." Replied MacLeod in his deep Scottish accent. "I've been lookin' o'er yon plans o' theirs and it's mad, I tell ya,' mad!"

"Tell me what you really think, Jessie." Smiled Harrow as he joined MacLeod to look over the map. For a split second, the Scotsman remained stony faced before the jest sunk in and he gave a broad grin, which was pretty difficult to see under all that facial hair.

"They want us to surface a mile from shore, correct?"

"Yip."

"And drop off a load o' pansies…"

"Commandos, Jessie. Commandos." Scolded Harrow.

"Aye, pansies."

"I really need to get you on an anger management course."

"Why? I can manage my anger fine, ma' sel."

"Why do I bother?" Asked Farrow shaking his head, "so what's wrong with their plan?"

"We're too exposed on the surface. That's what's wrong! What if one of those blasted E-boats decides to play?"

"Then, we play nice like mum taught us."

"Stop it, sur! Ye ken what a mean."

"Aye, I do." Replied Harrow putting on a terrible Scottish accent which only proceeded to poke the hornet's nest even more, which was the desired effect. MacLeod bit down on his bottom lip, the thing that he does, that Harrow had noticed in the past, when he is trying to control his temper. "We have no choice, Jessie. This has come down from the top and they've ticked all the boxes."

"Beg your pardon, Sur, but it's not their arses getting shot at!"

"Agreed."

For the next half an hour, the two men ran the numbers and various scenarios on paper, trying to work out any other way of achieving their objective. To their joint frustration, they found no other way. To this end, Farrow ordered main gun and anti-aircraft battery drills until he was satisfied. MacLeod volunteered to take charge. It was a comfort to Harrow's ears when he heard the Scotsman's dulcet tones berating some seaman for either being too slow or forgetting something. A rating brought him a cup of something black and hot. The rating assured him that it was coffee, but his taste buds questioned that description. But he drank it anyway, as he poured over the map and their notes.

At **2100** hours, the lorry carrying the soldiers and Fallon cleared the front gate and headed to the berth where HMS Spectre sat wallowing. A sentry on the gang plank challenged them and unslung his rifle.

"Stand down, Jacobs." Ordered a voice from the conning tower, it was Harrow. He swung one leg over and then the other, climbing down the foot holds in the tower. His feet made a reassuring thud as they hit the metal of the deck. He walked to the end of the gang plank just as Fallon reached it.

"Permission to come aboard, Sir?" Asked Fallon.

"Permission granted, Lieutenant."

"Fallon."

"Harrow."

The two men shook, and Harrow escorted him forward to the bow hatch. Harrow took a few moments to explain this was where the assault team would be disembarking. He pointed to the deck, explaining that it would be extremely slippery at that moment, as the submarine would be trying to stay as low in the water as possible in an attempt to not be spotted from the shore. Harrow also told Fallon that their time on the surface would be very limited, for that same reason. Fallon nodded.

"Excuse me, Sir." The two officers turned to see Sergeant Charlie Lawrie standing there. He saluted. "Where do we stow our gear?"

"Through this hatch Sergeant." Replied Harrow pointing to the hole in the deck.

"Very good, Sir." Lawrie turned, "right lads. Let's be havin' you!" The rest of the squad came on to the deck carrying two large black zip bags between six of them. The seventh member of the team was carrying three large army duffel bags which were making him sway from side to side. The two big bags were carefully manhandled through the hatch and then two other soldiers assisted the man with the duffel bags. Within the hour, all was set.

Fallon joined Harrow on the conning tower just as the Naval officer was about to give the command for the gang plank to be removed, a car came hurtling towards the dock with its lights on full, blaring it horn.

"Who's this blithering idiot?" Asked Harrow. Fallon did not have to reply as he knew it could only be one person, much to his annoyance. Now, the reason for Fallon's reaction to the arrival, to be clear, is rooted in the stories his father told him about this person. Also, you have to remember that, because his father was part of the Office of Special Projects, Fallon grew up with the inner circle of the organisation from Forrester down.

The car screeched to a halt, only a few feet away from the dock's edge, and an older man tumbled out. Gerald Cuthbertson, but instead of wearing his usual white technician's coat, the man was actually in uniform.

As Cuthbertson came on board, Fallon could make out the insignia of a Major on the epilates on the arrival's shoulders. Surely not. He waved a hand up at Fallon and then shouted something inaudible. He tried again but was drowned out by the noise coming from the vessels engines, which had started up.

He turned to one of the crew and said something to him, pointing as he did so back towards his car.

The crewman nodded and ran down the gang plank, over to the rear of the car, opened the boot and brought out another large duffel bag. He hurried back on the boat, plonking the bag at Cuthbertson's feet before saluting. Cuthbertson looked down at his own hand and then nervously returned the salute.

2130. HMS Spectre moved gracefully out of the harbour and into the channel that would take them out to sea. On the bridge, Harrow barked orders down one of two communication pipes, before lifting up the binoculars, which hung around his neck, and scanning ahead. He shouted another order down the other tube. Fallon just stood there, enjoying this part of the ride. Meanwhile, down in the bowels of the ship, just along from the small galley, Cuthbertson had been using his time wisely, unpacking his equipment that he had brought aboard. He had just laid it out on two tables as Fallon and Harrow entered. Harrow saluted the superior officer in the room whilst Fallon stifled a laugh.

"Poppycock." Said Cuthbertson at the formality of Harrow's greeting. Harrow looked mystified. "The rank is honorary, old chap. No need for ceremony here. Now down to business." Cuthbertson reached over and picked up a machine gun. "Gentlemen, let me introduce you to the Thompson M1A1 machine gun, courtesy of our American friends. It carries a twenty or thirty round magazine of point four five calibre ammo." He then picked up an automatic pistol that Fallon recognised from his field training. The Colt 1911A1. He reached over and picked one up.

To him, it was like welcoming an old friend home. "The Colt 1911A1 carries a point four five bullet in a clip that holds seven of the little blighters." The equipment officer handed his one to Harrow to try. "There we have it, Gentlemen, your two main weapons of defence and attack. I also have a few boxes of grenades and something the Americans are calling plastique."

He reached into the bag and brought out a block of something resembling children's modelling clay. "You can mould this stuff into any shape." He tossed it towards Fallon who snapped at it, giving the technician a worried look like a rabbit caught in a set of car headlights. "Relax, K-12. It is perfectly safe until you add the timing pencil, then the fireworks start."

He looked gleefully at the two men looking for recognition that he had cracked a funny. They either had not noticed or were ignoring him. Anyhow, he continued the briefing by explaining the contents of the two large bags that had caused so much bother when they were being loaded.

They were Goatley collapsible boats. These handy little devices could be assembled in around two minutes and had wooden bottoms and canvas sides. Each boat could carry up to ten men but only weighed three hundred and thirty pounds (one hundred and fifty kilograms) each, which meant two men could carry and assemble them with relative ease.

"It seems like you've thought of everything, Major Cuthbertson." Commented Harrow laying the Colt back down.

"I do try, old boy. I do try." Fallon was sure, that if Cuthbertson's head got any bigger it would surely explode. The mental picture of this, for some reason, brought a smile to his face. Smithers looked over with a 'care to share' look on his face but Fallon shook his head. Some thoughts were best kept private.

Outside, the dark shape of the submarine slipped silently below the surface. A whistle like a kettle boiling caught Harrow's attention. He walked over to the communication pipe.

"Captain."

"We've just dived Sir." Informed the dulcet tones of MacLeod.

"Take her down to two hundred feet and hold her steady."

"Aye, Captain."

The boat began to creak and complain. Whilst his two companions looked at each other with concerned looks on their faces, Harrow seemed not to be bothered and continued to look over the rest of the equipment. It was going to be a long boring trip across the Channel as the submarine had to remain submerged and thus, travel slower than she would have on the surface.

Fallon and the rest of the assault team took full advantage of this down time, resting where they could. Cuthbertson, on the other hand, decided to walk about the boat annoying people with questions about how the equipment they were using worked, like a kid in a candy store. It was nearly dawn when Harrow gently shook Fallon's shoulder.

"I'm awake." Fallon announced yawning.

"Good because we've arrived at your drop off point." Informed Harrow helping Fallon to his feet.

"The rest of the men?"

"Ready, and awaiting your orders."

"Thanks, Geordie." The two men exchanged brief smiles before moving forward to the bridge. Harrow went over to the periscope; he picked up a pair of gloves and put them on.

"Periscope depth." Harrow ordered swinging his cap around so the peak of it was down the back of his neck. Everyone felt the boat rise, leaving their stomachs behind like you do during a ride in an elevator.

"Periscope depth, Sir." Announced MacLeod pressing a button on the side of the scope's housing. The periscope moved upwards, as Harrow, beginning in a squat, rose with the machine to fully upright. He scanned the surroundings moving through a full 360° range of movement.

"Down scope."

"Well?" Asked Fallon.

"All quiet." Smiled Harrow, "surface!"

HMS Spectre rose to the surface like a huge dark sea monster. Within seconds, the hatches were opened and there was a hive of activity out on the housing. The commandos hauled their boats up onto the housing and began assembling them. Several of the crew acted as both lookouts and gunners, scanning the horizon for any sign of a threat.

When the men spoke, they did so in whispers or used hand signals to get their points across. Harrow looked down at a stopwatch that he had started as soon as he came up on deck. The soldiers finished their crafts and loaded them with equipment before easing them over the side. They clambered aboard and waited for Fallon who had just arrived on deck. He saluted Harrow and mouthed the word 'thanks' before getting into the second boat.

"Wait! Wait!" Yelled a man's voice from the top of the conning tower. It was Cuthbertson.

"Will you be quiet!" Hissed Harrow.

"Oh, sorry old chap! Got a bit carried away." Cuthbertson whispered climbing down the ladder and standing on the wet deck looking from one boat to the other and back.

"What the hell do you think you're doing?" Hissed Fallon.

"I'm coming with you."

"Like hell you are!"

"Orders, my dear Fallon. Orders." Said Cuthbertson.

"Who's?" Fallon already knew the answer but needed it confirmed.

"The Colonel."

"Damn it!" Cursed Fallon punching the water.

"Why?"

"Because you need someone to dispose of the LD-27 and I'm your man."

"Really?"

"Do I have to pull rank, Lieutenant?" Asked Cuthbertson. Fallon shook his head and offered him a helping hand to get into his boat. After a couple of failed attempts and a guiding shove from Lawrie, Cuthbertson's butt connected with the plank of wood that served as both a seat and ribbing for the boat.

"See you in six hours." Fallon whispered. Harrow nodded as the boats pushed off heading towards the beach. Once they had gotten far enough away, with a hiss of air and bubbles of water, like the monster exhaling, the submarine sank beneath the waves once more.

"K-12."

"Yes, Sparks?"

"Did you notice the sign above the periscope?"

"No, can't say I did." Said Fallon honestly.

"It said, failure is not an option."

"That sounds vaguely familiar." Commented Fallon with a wry smile on his face.

"Yes. Doesn't it but I can't place where I've either seen it or heard it before."

"Don't give yourself an aneurism, Sparks. Try and concentrate on the job at hand." Suggested Fallon as he began to row using one of the four paddles that came with the boats. Their arms certainly got a workout, as did their backs. They were huffing and puffing by the time they made landfall, each man jumping from the boat into knee deep water and hauling their respective boat ashore.

Three of the soldiers made a security perimeter facing up the beach with weapons drawn. The others set to dismantling the boats and stashing them behind some rocks before they covered them with sand. Satisfied, Fallon motioned to Lawrie to come over and they went over the plan.

"I want you to take Alpha section up the road and cut the telephone lines so the chateau is cut off and can't summon help." Lawrie nodded. "It will also be your job to cover me and Bravo section's escape from the chateau." Again, the Sergeant nodded but then froze as the sound of footsteps scrunching on the shingle further up the beach alerted the men that they were about to have a visitor or visitors. They threw themselves to the ground, drawing their weapons and trying to keep as low to the ground as possible. The footsteps stopped and a flashlight came on. Then off and then on once more.

"Monsieur, are you there?" Whispered a French voice that Fallon recognised as the jovial moustached man from his previous visit. Fallon, still cautious, stood up slowly but signalled for the rest of his men to stay prone.

"The phoenix dies…" He said into the haze of the early morning.

"…But rises again in the flames." Came the correct response, and the large round shape of the moustached man came into view, over one of the dunes. He waved. Fallon walked up and greeted him with a gentlemanly handshake, but the big man was having none of that stiff upper lip rubbish, and grabbed him, putting him into a bear hug, almost squeezing the life out of him, before kissing him on both cheeks, the traditional French greeting.

He put Fallon back down just as the rest of the Commandos got to their feet. Flustered, Fallon made the introductions. The Frenchman did the rounds, warmly shaking each man's hand, welcoming them to his country.

"Where's Dianne and Phillippe?" Fallon asked once the introductions had died down. The moustache man's smile disappeared, and when he spoke, he almost wailed with sorrow.

"They have been taken, Monsieur."

"Taken? Where?" Asked Fallon alarmed.

"Firstly, to the chateau…"

"And then?" The moustached man hesitated. Fallon grabbed the man by the shoulders and shook him hard, his frustration clear for all to see. Cuthbertson stepped forward and put a calming hand on the young man's shoulder. He looked back at Cuthbertson, his eyes wide with terror. The older man smiled and shook his head gently.

"Give the man a chance, old boy." Said the older man as he released his grip on Fallon's shoulder. "Take a breath."

Fallon suddenly realised what he was doing and immediately released his own grip, apologising as he did so. He took a step back before he spoke again. "Where did they take them next?"

"Phillippe. Nowhere. He is dead at the hands of the Germans at the chateau. Dianne, I do not know."

"What do you mean, you don't know?" Fallon could feel the frustration boiling up inside of him again like a volcano about to spew magma.

"She has been taken." The moustache man looked up to the heavens, as if he were trying to get divine help to assist him tell the next part. He wailed like a banshee as he continued, "the Gestapo have her, Monsieur, over in the next town!"

"How long?" Fallon asked deflated, like someone had just sucker punched him in the gut.

"At least ten days."

A mixture of shock and hopelessness appeared on Fallon's face. Instantly, after hearing the news, he started to waver, doubting his decisions. One minute, it was we should do this, and then in the same breath, do you think that it is right, or he would go off on a completely different tangent. Cuthbertson stepped forward.

"Gentlemen, we would all agree the news about our friends is shocking, but this must not divert our attention, to our primary objective." He looked around the group to gauge their reaction. On the whole, everyone was agreeing accept Fallon, who just looked ahead blankly.

"Sergeant Lawrie, take half the men and carry out your mission." Lawrie pointed to three men, they grabbed their equipment and started trudging up the beach towards the road.

"Monsieur, one moment." Said the moustached man. He whistled and as if he had used a magic wand, several men appeared on the crest of the dune. "Mes amis."

"Better late than never, my jovial friend." Said Cuthbertson welcoming the addition to the group. "I want half your friends to go with the Sergeant and half to stay with us." Moustache translated and the men dispersed accordingly.

The newcomers were armed with a mixture of weapons. MP-40s, stolen from the Germans, bolt action rifles that looked like leftovers from the First War and

British Sten guns. "K-12!" Cuthbertson shouted. "K-12!" He repeated.

Fallon stood motionless, just staring into nothingness. Cuthbertson stepped in front of him and slapped him hard across the face. It must have stung because Cuthbertson winced. He raised his hand again to strike but Fallon blocked it.

"Enough." He hissed. "I'm back."

"About bloody time. We need someone to take charge."

"You seemed to be doing alright." Fallon commented with a slight smile.

"Not used to it, old boy." Came the relieved reply.

Fallon gathered the remaining men around him in a circle and drew a rough outline of the chateau in the sand, pointing out the machine gun nests at the entrance and the various guard positions. Each of these will have to be dealt with before they enter the building itself. These were their main priorities.

Everyone agreed. Cuthbertson had slinked off and unearthed a medium sized bag from where the boats had been buried. In all the hubbub, he had mistakenly buried the bag instead of leaving it out. He put the carrying strap around his neck. Fallon looked over at him raising an eyebrow but was answered by just a single thumbs up. Fallon cocked his head briefly before carrying on.

15 – A Wee Surprise

" **A** wee surprise for the Germans." Hinted Cuthbertson as he caught up when they moved off. Fallon was going to press him more about the contents of the bag but thought he would wait and see what was in Cuthbertson bag of tricks.

The moustache man had kindly laid on a couple of farm trucks for them to use, battered and smelling of manure, with strands of straw poking up through the boards in the floor in the back. They would have to suffice, otherwise, the six hours allocated for the mission, would be eaten up just getting to the target. They stopped about a mile from the chateau and Fallon looked at his watch. By his reckoning, Alpha should be in the process of cutting the telephone lines about now, as well as setting up a defensive position to cover his team's escape.

Sure enough, three miles away, two commandos had shimmied up the telephone poles and using wire cutters, had managed to cut the chateau off from the outside World. The next job was the defensive position. Lawrie positioned two of his men further up the road as lookouts, whilst two others set up a browning machine gun post, one acting as the gunner and the other feeding in the bullets via a belt from an ammunition box. Their positioning gave them a good view of the road in front of them, or field of fire to use the military vernacular. Happy, Lawrie signalled for the rest of his party to fan out on both sides of the road using the ditches that paralleled it as cover.

Meanwhile, Bravo had made its way to within a hundred yards of the chateau. Fallon took out a set of binoculars and looked at the target. All was strangely quiet, which worried him. A couple of guards, positioned on one of the machine gun nests, were sitting on top of the sandbag wall, smoking cigarettes, and happily chewing the fat with each other, laughing, and joking.

A Sergeant came out of the guard hut and Fallon thought the two sentries would get a roasting from him but no, he joined in. What the hell was going on? He panned round to where the trucks had been parked on his first visit. They were gone. Where were the trucks? He motioned for Cuthbertson to come forward and handed him the binoculars, pointing as Cuthbertson took them towards the empty parking bay and the doors that lead to the rear of the chateau.

"There's nothing there, old chap. What am I supposed to be looking at?" Asked a mystified Cuthbertson.

"Exactly. The trucks have gone, and we need to find out where the hell they've gone!" With a forward movement of his arm, Bravo moved slowly forward, weapons drawn and grenades at the ready. They were on the machine gun nests before the Germans knew what had hit them. With short bursts from the Thompsons, the sergeant and his two comrades were easily and quickly dispatched. BOOM! BOOM! BOOM! Exploded three grenades that one of the Frenchmen had tossed into the second nest and the guard hut.

Two of the Frenchmen stood in the doorway of the hut and sprayed the interior with bullets. The alarm sounded and men rushed from their billets like ants from an ant hill, straight into a hail of lead, most of them did not stand a chance.

Others were able to give off a few short bursts from their MP-40s before falling. Fallon signalled for two of his commandos to set up their own machine gun nest using one of the captured German Mausers, only one was still operational, covering the approach road. Suddenly, after the chaos of the last five minutes, there was a deathly silence. Then CRACK! One of the Frenchmen fell dead. CRACK! And a round kicked up a small plume of dust in front of Fallon's feet before he dived for cover.

"Sniper!" Someone yelled as they all took cover, the best they could, everyone's eyes looking for the tell-tale glint from the barrel or the sight. CRACK! Another man bit the dust, but the rifle shot was answered by some rounds from a couple of the machine guns, returning fire. Fallon looked up and saw the bullets slamming into the parapet that ran along the top of the building.

He signalled to one of the commandos to lob a grenade in that direction. BOOM! Fallon gingerly stood up ready to be felled by the sniper. Nothing. He urged his remaining men to move forward. They went up the stairs and stopped outside the closed main doors. Hugging the wall on either side, the men waited as Fallon slowly turned the handle.

A machine gun fired from the other side, peppering the door with holes, and Fallon with splinters. He looked over at the first soldier and held up three fingers. He counted down to one and then signalled for a grenade to be thrown. The soldier nodded, unclipping a device from his belt.

Fallon mouthed the count down and then turned the handle, pushing the door open just enough to allow the grenade to be thrown. They took cover just as the explosive went off. Fallon opened the door fully to see a young officer lying there in a pool of his own blood. He recognised him as Hauptmann Schumann, the General's Aide.

Bravo fanned out, searching the ground floor, opening a door, tossing a grenade before entering and spraying the room with gunfire. Once the ground floor had been cleared, they repeated the procedure for the second floor. No sign of Altman.

"Sir!" Shouted one of the commandos. He had found the door leading to the basement. One soldier opened it slowly whilst another tossed a grenade. They waited for it to detonate before slowly moving down the stairs, one step at a time. The corridor opened up in front of them and each man pinned themselves to either wall, edging slowly along with weapons raised. CRACK! Went a pistol shot but the bullet buried itself harmlessly into the wall.

"General Altman!" Shouted Fallon, "give up. You have nowhere to go."

"Schlange, is that you?"

"It's not Schlange, Sir. It's Fallon."

"Ah, so my mysterious Major returns."

"Affirmative, Sir. Please put your weapon down, and come out. I promise you will be treated fairly."

"Why should I? Anyway, you're too late. They have all gone." Announced Altman from somewhere down the corridor.

"Gone, Sir. Where?" Asked Fallon moving quietly forward.

"Trucks. Many trucks..."

"Where did they go, General?"

"To a ship and then on to victory."

Fallon looked over to Cuthbertson who tapped his right temple with his index finger signalling that Altman had lost his mind. "What was the name of the ship, Sir?"

"Our last chance. Our last chance!" Altman yelled bursting from the room at the end of the corridor and bellowing like a madman. He fell in a hail of bullets as several machine guns opened up a storm of death upon him. Fallon rushed forward, kicking the Luger automatic across the floor out of reach, he knelt down beside Altman.

"Where is the girl?"

"How nice, the spy in love with the tramp." Coughed Altman, blood pouring from his mouth.

"Where is she, you bastard?" Said Fallon through clenched teeth, shaking him. Altman laughed and then his body went limp. He was gone, but Fallon continued to shake him as it that would revive him long enough to answer. Cuthbertson put a hand on his shoulder.

"He's gone." Was all Cuthbertson said, before moving forward into the room that Altman had come from. He searched the room and then came out. "The stuff's not here."

"Burn it!" Said Fallon coldly, as he got to his feet. "Burn it all!" He turned and walked back up the corridor as the commandos and Cuthbertson unpacked the plastic explosives and the time pencils.

With the explosives set in strategic places, Bravo made a hasty retreat to the main gate and just in time. The first explosion blew the rear doors off, and the rest exploded in succession, like some rolling storm of devastation. Eventually, the whole building erupted into a huge fireball sending the members of Bravo diving for cover, as a hail of debris came raining down on them.

Job done, Bravo climbed back onto the trucks and headed towards their rendezvous with Alpha. As they rounded the corner, they could hear the sound of gunfire. They disembarked from the trucks and moved forward on foot.

Ahead, Alpha had engaged a German patrol which consisted of two trucks, a Kubelwagen, containing an SS Major, and a halftrack. Grenades were being thrown as Bravo arrived, but the explosives fell short, detonating on the road, but managing to take out four infantry men.

The Browning machine gun chattered into life, but the bullets simply pinged off the heavy armour of the halftrack, as it started to rumble forward, the gunner opening up with the machine gun mounted above the driver's position.

Fallon witnessed two of Alpha fall before his team joined in the fight. The Major hid behind the rear of his vehicle, egging on his troops to move forward and engage. The commandos were losing the fight and started to give up ground as they began to fall back to where the trucks were. Then a strange sound joined in with the orchestral symphony of battle.

A whoomphing sound. And again. Whoomph! The sound emanated from behind Fallon. Seconds later, the halftrack exploded in a ball of fire. The men inside screaming as they were engulfed in flame. The gunner, his body now a human torch, came running from the rear of the vehicle only to be shot by one of the Frenchmen.

Realising the tide of the battle had changed, the Germans soldiers stood up, throwing their weapons to the ground, and raising their hands in surrender. All of them except the Major, who yelled at them from the back of his vehicle, before falling quiet. He, too, stood up with his hands raised, tossing his side arm into the dirt before moving to join the rest of the prisoners.

Behind him came Sergeant Lawrie, his automatic pointed in the Major's direction. He nodded towards Fallon, who smiled, relieved that, at least this part was over. Cuthbertson came to stand beside him, and Fallon looked down at what he was carrying. It looked like a pipe with several chambers attached to a handle with a trigger.

"Meet the CP-8 rocket launcher." Announced Cuthbertson, "I've been dying to try this wee beauty out!" He admitted, his face beaming with pride.

"Your little surprise for the Germans?" Asked Fallon.

"Yip." Smiled Cuthbertson, the grin almost cutting his face into two hemispheres.

"God help us!" Said Fallon shaking his head as he walked over to the Major who was sitting on the ground, with his hands clasped behind his head. "Where did the Gestapo take the local girl, Herr Major?"

"What local girl?" Replied the Major, pleading ignorant.

"Let me ask you again!" Hissed Fallon grabbing the CP-8 from Cuthbertson.

"Fallon!" Protested Cuthbertson.

"Now, I don't know what this contraption will do to a human body, especially at close range, but you will agree, it made one hell of a mess of your little halftrack." He pointed the weapon at the Major's head. "Where is the girl?"

"You wouldn't. It is against the Geneva Convention."

Fallon pressed the barrel of the weapon hard against the officer's forehead, so hard that it made the man cry out. "I won't ask you again." The Major looked into Fallon's eyes and only saw darkness. Crazy eyes. Fallon's mother had called it, when he returned home, after being expelled from school, after he was involved in a fight with the school bully.

"She is being held in the town hall a few kilometres from here. Interrogator Frettchen and his dog, Wiesel, have been questioning her about you. She is not in very good shape." A sick smile came over the Major's face, one of satisfaction.

Fallon used the butt of the weapon to disperse the emotion, striking him across the face, knocking him to the ground. The Major picked himself up, wiping the blood from his mouth before retaking his seated position. "You all saw that!" He yelled towards the assembled group. "He struck an unarmed man, this animal!"

"I saw nothing, mate." Replied Lawrie as he walked away.

"Strip." Ordered Fallon.

"Pardon me?" Asked the Major, scarcely believing his ears.

"I said STRIP!" Yelled Fallon knocking the officer's hat to the ground. "Get them all to strip! It's time we paid the Gestapo a visit."

Once out of uniform, the Germans were loaded up into a truck under armed guard. The commandos became the infantrymen whilst Lawrie and Cuthbertson became the officers, Cuthbertson trading like for like. Fallon thought he suited the SS uniform and nodded his approval. Fallon remained in his uniform.

"What's the plan, Sir?" Asked Lawrie.

"Simple. Frettchen wants Louis Serpens...so why don't we give him what he wants, but on our terms, not his." Said Fallon. He walked around to the boot of the vehicle, opened it and stowed the suitcase before climbing into the rear of the Kubelwagen with Cuthbertson, as Lawrie got in the front with one of the commandos. The engine started after the third attempt. Fallon ordered for the prisoners to be taken to the rendezvous site while they headed off to try and rescue Dianne.

16 – Into the Ferret's Lair

The Kubelwagen containing Fallon, Cuthbertson and the two commandos coughed and spluttered its way into Abbeville, clearly suffering from the numerous bullet holes evident in the bodywork. It came into the town square and then died. Lawrie climbed out and opened the hood. After a brief inspection, he slammed the hood down.

"Kaput."

"Great." Cursed Fallon as he and Cuthbertson climbed out the back of the vehicle. "Lawrie, I want you to acquire us another mode of transport and have it ready for our departure."

"Yes, Sir."

"Sparks...sorry I mean SS-Strumbannfuhrer...take me to your leader."

Cuthbertson coughed nervously as he unholstered his sidearm, a Walther P-38 automatic, and pushed Fallon forward. "Move you dog!" Yelled Cuthbertson and then whispered in Fallons ear, "I could get to like this."

"Don't overdo it, Herr Major." Fallon pleaded.

"Halt!" Ordered a voice. Cuthbertson and Fallon turned around to see a Corporal walking towards them. "What is going on here?" He asked.

"I am Major Schlange and I have apprehended the fugitive Serpens. The one that Interrogator Frettchen is looking for."

"Where is the rest of your convoy, Herr Strumbannfuhrer?" Asked the Corporal suspiciously.

"We were engaged in a firefight with this dog's resistance group...as if you take a look at the state of my car, it will bare testament to it."

"But Herr..." Began the NCO.

"I don't know what it is like in the Wehrmacht but in the SS, it is customary to salute a superior officer." Cuthbertson remarked. Realising his serious breach in decorum, the NCO snapped to attention and up went his arm.

"Heil Hitler!"

"Heil Hitler!" Said Cuthbertson, "return to your duties and I will make a point in mentioning your attention to duty to Herr Frettchen."

"Danke, Herr Strumbannfuhrer."

"By the way, where is Herr Frettchen?"

"In the main hall, just across there, Herr Strumbannfuhrer." Pointed the NCO to a nondescript building across the square with large swastikas hanging from the eaves. Cuthbertson saluted and pushed Fallon in the direction of the building.

"You enjoyed that." Whispered Fallon once the NCO had gone.

"Yes." Agreed Cuthbertson with a smile as he gave Fallon an extra shove.

"Steady on." Reminded Fallon, "don't get carried away with your part."

"Oh sorry. I'm kinda new at this spy business." Apologised Cuthbertson, Fallon gave him a disbelieving look that made him correct himself, "the field work anyway."

They made their way up the stairs past another couple of guards who saluted the Major. Cuthbertson nodded, but then gave the correct response, thanks, in no small part, to a cough from his prisoner. They entered the building. The main hall was decked out in Nazi bunting and a large picture of Adolf Hitler took centre stage on the wall opposite the entrance.

After a brief discussion with a guard sitting at the reception desk, the two of them made their way down to the cellar. A sickly smell greeted them as they went down deeper. Musky. A dampness mixed with god knows what. The two of them made their way down the wooden stairs, which creaked with every footstep. Once at the bottom, they were greeted with a long corridor that seemed to run underneath and away from the building.

No doubt an addition made by the current occupiers. Barred cells flanked the corridor. The smell changed from dampness to what could only be described as indescribable. A sense of despair and hopelessness. Out of each cell came moans belonging to the lost and the forgotten. Fallon struggled to maintain both his dignity and his cover. He looked back to Cuthbertson who, too, was clearly having issues. A baptism of fire for both of them, it would seem.

The corridor was torch lit and the flames danced, aided by an unknown wind. Shadows licked and bent along the stone walls, highlighting each crack and hole, as if they were acting out some macabre play for an unseen audience. It was as if they had entered a medieval castle and had found their way down into its dungeons. To add to the effect, a rat scurried in front of Fallon, who jumped back. Cuthbertson glanced across at him with a smirk on his face. Fallon just glared at him and proceeded to walked along the corridor, once more.

Cuthbertson's curiosity overtook him when passing a door on his left. It was wooden like the others, but something drew him to it, like a moth to a naked flame. He stopped outside it. There was a small inspection hatch level with his face. He reached for the small latch holding it close, and opened it. He lent forward to allow his eyes to look it and he recoiled in horror. Inside, was sparsely decorated. In fact, there was only a chair on which stood a man, scantily dressed, his body covered with cuts and bruises.

What startled Cuthbertson was the positioning of the man. He stood with his arms stretched out behind him, his wrists secured by a rope but with a slight gap between his wrists to allow a meat hook to be attached, which was, in turn, connected to another piece of rope which was then looped around one of the beams in the roof. As far as Cuthbertson could make out, which was difficult to see because the room on the other side of the door was dimly lit, there was a bit of give in the rope hanging from the ceiling but not a lot.

"I see the Strumbannfuhrer has stumbled upon one of our interrogation rooms." Said a voice from further up the corridor. Fallon and Cuthbertson turned to see a Corporal approaching them. He saluted Cuthbertson who, naturally, returned it, even though he was sickened to his very core.

"Who is it?" Inquired Cuthbertson.

"A simple peasant." Replied the soldier, his voice oozing contempt with every word.

"What has he done to warrant such punishment?"

"He's French." Came the blunt reply.

"How long is he going to be left like that?"

"Until he weakens…"

"And then what?"

"He falls off the stool."

Cuthbertson looked at the soldier, giving him one of those unmistakeable looks that told the subordinate to expand on his previous statement.

"Ach so…the wretch will fall, and his shoulders will dislocate."

"And what if he doesn't?"

"Fall?"

Cuthbertson nodded.

"Then, we add to the fun…" Replied the soldier, as if he was describing his favourite party game to a friend. "We tie a noose around his neck and assist him along the way…"

"How?"

The soldier made a side swipe with his foot suggesting that they would kick away the stool and then he simulated someone being hung, a guttural sound coming from his mouth as if he was choking. The mere thought of this barbaric action made both Fallon and Cuthbertson want to throw up. Cuthbertson, himself, put his hand to his mouth to stop himself from doing just that into his mouth.

"Is the Strumbannfuhrer feeling alright?" Asked the concerned soldier. "Perhaps our methods don't meet with your approval, Sir?"

Cuthbertson waved the comment off.

"Bad oysters at one of the local cafes." He lied.

"Ach so. If the Strumbannfuhrer will excuse me?"

Cuthbertson nodded. The two saluted and the soldier walked off down the corridor.

"If your explosives work Cuthbertson both him and that poor bastard in the cell will be put out of their misery." Comforted Fallon.

"Yes...yes...quite."

The duo went to the end, that suddenly opened up into a larger well lit room, the lighting coming from bulbs in the ceiling. A chair sat in the middle. It was empty. A table off to the left had various tools laid out on it, the kind you would use for woodwork, but they doubted this was their function here. Some of them carried blood stains on them while others, like the plyers, had what looked like human tissue embedded in the teeth. A scream from another room focused their attention. The two of them headed to the source.

A wooden door separated them from the room next door. Cuthbertson turned the handle and slowly pushed it open. It creaked. The horror in front of them made them gasp with shock. Dianne was there, right enough, but suspended from a hook in the ceiling, via a rope looped around it and tied to her wrists, her feet dangling about a foot from the floor. Her body twisted and battered. Bruises upon bruises. Her once beautiful face now more like a gargoyle carved in the towers of Notre Dame Cathedral. Grotesque and misshapen. Her nose clearly broken.

Two rivulets of dried blood tracing paths down and over her lips. Her right eye was swollen and closed, with her left not far behind. Fallon and Cuthbertson entered just as the brute Wiesel landed a right hook into her side. She moaned and her body swung slightly under the force of the blow. Wiesel stopped and looked towards the arrivals.

"Can I help you, Gentlemen?" Asked a voice. Frettchen came out of the shadows.

"Err…yes. My name is Schlange. SS-Strumbannfuhrer Schlange." Introduced Cuthbertson, saluting. Frettchen saluted back as he glided phantom-like across the floor and sat down on a wooden chair opposite Dianne. "I have apprehended the enemy agent you have been looking for, Herr Frettchen."

"Ach so." Frettchen got to his feet and walked over to Fallon. He reached out and grasped Fallon's jaw with his right hand, digging his fingers deep into his jaw as he moved it from left to right, examining him like you would do for an animal at an auction before purchasing it. Then, without warning, he punched Fallon in the stomach, the blow dropping him to his knees. Winded, Fallon tried to get up but was felled by another blow across the side of his face. "You have done well, Herr Strumbannfuhrer. The Fuhrer will hear of the service you have done for the Reich." Purred Frettchen.

This time, Fallon was allowed to get to his knees without any retribution, spitting blood from his mouth. Wiesel laughed deeply, the kind of noise you would hear if you laughed into an empty barrel. Fallon whispered something. "What did you say, dog?" Asked Frettchen. Fallon repeated it, again as a whisper. Frettchen bent down to get a clearer listen.

"Woof!" Said Fallon as he heads butted Frettchen and breaking his bonds. Wiesel, momentarily taken by surprise by the move, quickly regained his wits, and lumbered towards Fallon, but stopped as a whistle rang out. Wiesel turned and saw Cuthbertson standing there with his silenced Walther drawn.

Cuthbertson fired twice, catching Wiesel once in the chest, and once in the forehead, the oak of a man fell forward, crashing into the chair sending splinters everywhere. Cuthbertson tossed Fallon the still smoking automatic as he went across and tried to untie Dianne. After a couple of attempts, he looked despairingly at Fallon. Fallon prodded Frettchen with the barrel of the automatic.

"Help him, or I'll kill you."

"Then, kill me."

"Don't tempt me, you bastard!" Threatened Fallon, "help him with her." He motioned to Cuthbertson with the barrel of the gun. Frettchen reluctantly got to his feet, blood streaming from his nose. He wiped away some of the crimson liquid with the back of his shirt sleeve before assisting Cuthbertson to unhook Dianne, who flopped to the floor in a heap.

"There. She is down. Now what?"

"She's in a bad way." Said a concerned Cuthbertson. He untied her hands and draped one arm over his shoulder. "She needs urgent help." Fallon nodded as he started to follow Cuthbertson out of the room. Frettchen shouted after them.

"What happens to me? Are you going to leave me like this?"

Fallon turned and smiled before closing the door behind him, the bolt sliding across the door gave him a warm feeling. He reached into his pocket and pulled out a small brick of plastique explosive from inside his tunic and some wire. He placed the brick about three feet away from the door, wedging it between two pillars. He tied one end of the wire to the door and the other he imbedded it into the plastique. This end also had a detonation fuse attached.

The hope being that Frettchen would be in a hurry to catch up with his prey, fuming at being humiliated and his haste would be his undoing. He would pull the door open, and the detonator would explode the plastique. Fallon checked the tension on the wire before running to catch up with Cuthbertson, taking Dianne's other arm and looping it around his neck. Their pace quickens considerably. The guard in the hall came forward to investigate just as the three of them emerged from the cellar.

"What is going on?" He asked as he unshouldered his MP-40 machine gun.

"These prisoners have been ordered to be transported to the waiting car outside by Herr Frettchen for interrogation back in Paris." Said Cuthbertson.

"But why is the man untied?" The MP-40 was now levelled at them.

"Do you really think an officer of the Reich would soil himself with the blood of these scum!" Replied a disgusted Cuthbertson, with an air of pomposity in his voice. The MP-40 lowered slightly as the guard smiled. Fallon faked a stumble and the guard moved closer to assist him back to his feet. The Walther fired once, catching the soldier in the chest, he turned and dropped to the floor. Cuthbertson propped a dazed Dianne up in a vacant chair before helping Fallon undress the soldier before the blood spoiled the uniform.

Minutes later, an SS-Strumbannfuhrer and a Wehrmacht Corporal helped the battered body of a Marquis female into the back of a Kubelwagen that someone had parked thoughtfully close to the entrance. Cuthbertson got into the back beside her and pulled the seat back. Fallon hurriedly got in the front and started the engine.

Meanwhile, down in the cellar, Frettchen tried the door handle and was surprised by the fact that it was unlocked. He yanked the door open and was about to break into a run when something caught his attention, the wire between the pillars. Frettchen just had enough time to run back in, and duck behind the table before the plastique exploded. His expletive was drowned out by the detonation. Sirens went off as men scurried about the square like ants, their attention focused on the main building and not the staff car that was driving away from the scene.

Frettchen staggered from the building, his face blooded, his uniform torn. He yelled at a couple of soldiers who ran in front of him, ordering him to get his staff car and organise some outriders. They saluted and hurried off to carry out his orders. Moments later, the Mercedes Benz belonging to Frettchen was speeding out of the square, preceded by two motorcycles with sidecars, each with Mauser submachine guns mounted on the cowled of the sidecar.

A lorry containing half a dozen troops followed at the rear. Beside the Gestapo officer sat Oberleutnant Frenz, his back poker straight, his voice like a broken record, continually thanking his superior for the opportunity to hunt down the saboteurs. Frettchen nodded and smiled the type of smile that told anyone who took the time to analyse his facial expression, showed that he was simply tolerating the young officer but barely.

Frenz's blonde hair and blue eyes were straight out of the Nazis handbook for the ideal Aryan. Ideologically brainwashed into thinking he was superior in all things. He looked down with disdain on anyone who did not match up to the blueprint his superiors in Berlin had laid out for him whilst he was being indoctrinated in school and at home. His mission in life was to be a good German and serve the Fatherland to the best of his ability and if required, pay the ultimate price for his allegiance to the Fuhrer, with his life. A twinkle in his eye and a tap on his holster only went to underline his eagerness to succeed.

Back in the lorry, Heimer, who was the NCO at the farmhouse to witness Frenz's greatest triumph to date, simply looked ahead. His eyes unblinking. Even when one of the soldiers asked him a question, it took several attempts to snap Heimer back from his train of thought. The veteran soldier's instincts were telling him that this pursuit was not going to end well. He hoped and prayed that he was wrong and that Frenz's glory hunting was not going to get some of his men killed. In the barracks, the common and garden soldier referred to Frenz in a particular way.

'*There goes 'no Frenz*', they would say commenting about the man's lack of companionship. The only warmth and comfort the man received was from the whores from the local brothel and he had to pay for that luxury and pay dearly. The local resistance used that very same house of ill repute as a source of intel on the enemies movements both sexually and militarily, thus keeping them one step ahead of them. Pillow talk seemed to loosen lips, making the Germans pay twice, once for a quick tumble between the sheets and then again when their patrols were ambushed by the resistance.

The Kubelwagen pulled its way around the bend in the road as Fallon floored the accelerator pedal. It was like trying to speed up a broken washing machine going up a hill in a mudslide. It was hopeless. For Fallon, it was hard to believe that what he was driving and trying extremely hard to keep on the road, was the military hybrid of the famous German automobile, the Volkswagen, or people's car.

The Kubelwagen essentially one of the world's first multi-terrain vehicles, with the engine in the rear, the added weight gave the vehicle more traction on difficult terrain, it was designed by that giant of the automotive field, Ferdinand Porsche, on the specific orders of Adolph Hitler to produce a low cost automobile that could house four people comfortably but cost no more than one thousand Reichsmarks to manufacture.

The result was the Volkswagen. The Beetle, as it would go on to be called, first came off the production line in Nineteen Thirty-Five, and would become one of the most popular types of car produced, becoming a major seller in the sixties and seventies.

Cuthbertson looked back and could see the approaching Germans. He reached forward and tapped Fallon on the shoulder. Fallon's head turned and Cuthbertson pointed backwards. Fallon nodded.

The sole of his boot now had no gap between it and the floor of the vehicle, Fallon was trying that hard to get every ounce of speed he could from the machine. They took another corner and then another. Gaining a slight distance advantage. They managed to get to the top of the slope which led to the beach and the awaiting boat from the submarine.

Fallon slammed on the breaks and quickly helped Cuthbertson lift Dianne up and over. Two sailors joined them, and Fallon ordered them to get to the boat and wait until the last possible moment for him. Cuthbertson and the sailors carried Dianne away leaving Fallon. He skipped around to the rear of the Kubelwagen and popped the boot, pulling out his suitcase. He climbed into the back of the vehicle where Dianne and Cuthbertson had been sitting only moments before and then tried to rack his brains as he tried to remember the sequence for arming the case.

"Turn the latches facing East to West and try to unlock it, it will detonate a small explosive device, thus destroying the contents and probably causing serious harm to the person opening it."

He could suddenly hear Cuthbertson' voice as clear as a bell, as if he was back at the OSP in London. He followed the instructions to the letter. CLICK! CLICK! Went the locks. Fallon lifted the lid slightly and left it like that, just enough to entice someone to investigate, like you would do with cheese to bait a mousetrap. He eased himself out of the vehicle and then ran to join the others. A few minutes after this the convoy appeared around the bend. The motorcycles slowed, the machine gunners in the sidecars arced their weapons towards the beach.

Frettchen screamed at the top of his voice for them to open fire. Immediately, popping sounds could be heard as two lines of yellow tracer bullets flicked and danced their way towards the retreating figures. The Mercedes and the truck stopped, both about fifty metres away from the stationary kubelwagen. Frettchen did not wait for his driver to get around and open the door, he flung it open and stepped out closely followed by Frenz, his mouth open with excitement, almost panting like the lap dog he was slowly becoming.

Frettchen pulled out his Walther P-38 automatic, and signalled to Heimer and his men to advance towards the stationary vehicle. Call it intuition, or a gut instinct, but Heimer felt uneasy about the whole current situation they found themselves facing and intentionally took his time organising his men, which infuriated Frettchen. The Gestapo officer bellowed, his face turning purple with rage.

Heimer saluted and went through the motions of hurrying his men along. Fed up waiting, Frenz, seeing an opportunity for glory and to impress the Gestapo officer, whispered something into his superior's ear, which made the Gestapo man nod his head in approval. Frenz stepped out from behind Frettchen, drew his Luger and strode forward towards the Kubelwagen.

He looked resplendent in his black Schutzstaffel, or SS, uniform with the silver lightning bolts on the collar. A marked contrast to the drabness of the feldgrau, or field grey, of the Wehrmacht soldiers under the command of Heimer. A couple of Heimer's men started to gather pace as they hastened towards the young officer's side but were quickly hauled back into line with a bark from Heimer.

Frenz reached the vehicle and studied it for a moment, walking cautiously around looking for anything out of the ordinary that would give a clue that it had been booby-trapped. He crouched down on his haunches and looked under the machine. Nothing stood out. As he stood back up to a vertical base, he saw it and it almost made his eyes pop out of his head. The scum had been careless and left a suitcase.

Immediately, his mind drifted towards pictures of him walking down a red carpet towards his beloved Fuhrer, saluting him, and then receiving an Iron Cross decoration, which the Fuhrer himself hung around his neck on a ribbon decorated with the swastika, the emblem of the party that he became a member of when he was old enough to walk.

That twinkle returned to his sky blue eyes as he stepped over and into the back of the vehicle. What treasures have they left behind? He asked himself as he knelt down in front of the suitcase. Perhaps plans of the next assault on his glorious Fatherland? A promotion hopefully awaited him. He reached forward, seizing the lid on either side. It was unlocked. He threw back the lid.

From the safety of their boat, Fallon and the others witnessed the explosion that tossed the vehicle up in the air like a ragdoll. The percussive force throwing Frettchen and the others onto their backs whilst the fireball engulfed both motorbikes, their fuel tanks erupting to add to the ferocity. The explosion rippled along the road, hitting each car in a procession of sheer destruction, the occupants not standing a chance of survival. This was how Frettchen met his end, engulfed in flame. Fallon glanced over to Cuthbertson, who was sitting up in the bow of the boat, a shocked look on his face.

"I thought you said, back at headquarters, that you only put a small amount of explosive in that case?"

"Artistic licence, dear boy. Artistic licence." Smiled Cuthbertson and turned his head back to facing forwards as if he had just bore witness to a fireworks display on Halloween and nothing more. They paddled out to the awaiting submarine and were helped aboard. Minutes later, the Spectre sank beneath the waves.

Horrifically, after the deaths of Frettchen, Frenz and the soldiers, the head of the SS in the area, SS-obergruppenführer und General der Waffen-SS Frederic Roetenberg, ordered the local populous to pay the price for this blatant act of terrorism. He ordered two villages closest to the scene to be rounded up, men, women and children. They were separated. The men and any male child over the age of fourteen, were herded into barns whilst the women and children were forced into the local churches. The doors were either locked or barred and then the soldiers fired into the buildings using whatever weapons that were available.

Pistols, machine guns and even Molotov cocktails made from wine bottles filled with gasoline and a lit rag stuffed in the mouth. The task of this retribution was given to the infamous Waffen SS or armed SS. They had already blooded themselves on the East Front and had left a trail of death and destruction in their wake as they came West.

Once the soldiers had ran out of ammunition or they thought all their captives were dead or dying, they set the buildings alight either with flamethrowers or by tossing in grenades. By seven that evening, with the buildings still ablaze, the troops withdrew to nearby school, halfway between the two villages and partied well into the night. Feasting on confiscated food, alcohol, and livestock. The next morning, with the embers of the churches and barns still smouldering, and still hungover from their festivities the night before, the Waffen SS returned to the scene of the massacres and raised both villages to the ground.

A squadron of six Panzer Mk IIIs lumbered their way into the centre of the villages, three in each, their seventy-five millimetre main guns being let loose on the buildings, whilst their seven point nine-two millimetre machine guns cut down any escapees. Soldiers equipped with anti-tank weapons, the panzerfaust 30, which consisted of a steel tube containing a propellant charge of gunpowder on which was screwed a grenade.

Others simply used stick grenades, tossing them into buildings as they either walked or drove past them, as if they were distributing candy to children. A month after the fact, a complaint is sent to the Berlin about the atrocity committed in the villages. The prefect of the area writes, in the strongest terms, demanding an investigation.

The SS sent one of their chief judges, who dined with Dietrich at his headquarters in a nearby chateau. The questioning is light and friendly, lasting several hours, much cognac was consumed. During which, Dietrich informs the investigator that the villages were hoarding weapons for the resistance, and the lawman takes this onboard. He reports back to his superiors that he is satisfied with the explanation and no further action needed to be taken.

The sickening thing is that none of the soldiers, or their commanders, were ever brought to trial, the exception being Roetenberg, who was apprehended during a routine sweep of the area by allied troops after the liberation of France. He was found trying to pass himself off as a lowly NCO of the Wehrmacht, or German army, hiding in a barn like a scared rat. He was recognised by one of the local partisans attached to the American patrol that had stumbled upon the group of soldiers quite by accident.

He would later be tried at the Nuremberg trials in 1946 for war crimes, and found guilty. He was hung in November of that same year. So, you could say, that a small measure of justice was brought upon the perpetrator but not enough to quell the loss of those relatives of the victims.

17 – Peenemunde

Back in London, a couple of days later, Forrester and Smithers looked over the intelligence the Fallon raid had gleaned. Two stacks of papers stood tall upon the desk the two men were standing behind. Dianne Gerard was recovering from her injuries in a local military hospital whilst the prisoners that Fallon had brought back were being interrogated in a Hotel complex the OSP use just for such events. The place has so many bugs in it that an exterminator would have an aneurysm. There were devices in the walls of the rooms, under the beds, in the telephones, and even in the toilets.

The favourite place to overhear conversations was the shower block at the rear of the property. On the surface, the place looked like your typical holiday destination if you discount the barbed wire curled around the top of the surrounding perimeter wall, the guard towers, with armed guards, and more patrolling the grounds with dogs pulling at their leashes.

Thanks to a combination of the eavesdropping at the 'Hotel,' work carried out by the code breakers at the super-secret Bletchley Park, and by simple leg work carried out by Forrester and his team, a plan was formulating.

"It would appear that the chateau was a front for the manufacture of this stuff called LD-27." Summarized Smithers as he walked across and looked at the pin board. It had aerial photographs of the chateau on it, pictures of Altman, and a man dressed in a white suit, whose identity for the moment, was unknown to them. "This man in the suit interests me, Sir." He continued pointing to the photograph with his pencil, "in all the pictures and by what Fallon has told me, seems to be the man in charge of the LD-27 operation."

"Agreed. But what about Altman? A puppet or willing contributor?" He opened an envelope and emptied the contents onto the desk. There was Altman's Iron Cross medal, his identification papers, and a ring that Fallon had found during a brief search of his desk. It was black with the number seventy-eight embossed on a circular frontage. "Setenta Ocho?"

Smithers nodded and added a picture of the ring to the board. He brought the end of the pencil up to his mouth and sucked on the rubberized end, thinking. He tapped the metal surround of the rubber on his teeth before turning to his superior. "Do we know where the LD-27 was being delivered to?" The question caused the two men to dive back into the folders, sifting through page upon page of information. Before the two of them knew it, the clock on Forrester's mantlepiece was chiming seven in the evening.

The two of them yawned and stretched. Forrester walked over to a small desk and poured himself a cup of coffee, the coffee from a tin and the hot water from the large metal urn that some kind orderly had assembled earlier. He lifted the mug in Smithers direction, who shook his head. A splash of milk and four sugars later, Forrester re-joined him at the table. They continued like this, well into the small hours of the morning, stopping to refill the mugs and to bite down on a selection of sandwiches that one of the WAAFs had left.

Forrester pulled open the blinds allowing in a blinding shaft of early morning light, which made both men shield their eyes.

"Jesus! What time is it?" Asked Forrester as he tied the strings that raised the blinds.

"A little after six, Sir." Informed Smithers looking at his wristwatch.

"What do we have?" Forrester said as he turned to the pin board, which they had been adding methodically to throughout the night, to the point they had stopped noticing what had been pinned to it. They each looked over their handywork. A knock came on the door and a Sergeant entered handing Forrester a piece of paper before leaving. "It would appear the chaps at Bletchley have picked up some chatter, on that Enigma machine thingy, about something codenamed 'Operation Storm' and a place called Peenemunde."

"Peenemunde?" Repeated Smithers almost running back to the table and frantically searching through a mound of files. Eventually finding what he was looking for, he came back to the board. "Peenemunde is on the Baltic Sea Island of Usedom in the Vorpommern-Griefswald district of Mecklenburg-Vorpormmern, Germany." The way he recited the information from the folder made Smithers sound like some kind of tour guide, then an officer in the intelligence corps.

He pulled out an aerial photograph of the island and pinned it to the board. "The boffins at the Ministry have been interested in this area for a while, as they're has been whispers of rocket testing being carried out there by this man...." He put another picture on the board showing a tall thin man in what looks like a business suit. "Wernher von Braun. A genius when it comes to rockets and propulsion."

"According to what I have here," interrupted Forrester, "activity has increased dramatically over the past fortnight with the expected special delivery from France."

"LD-27?"

"Possibly. Our sources say that the workforce is being nearly worked to death in preparation for the delivery."

"We need to find out two things..." Began Smithers looking at the aerial pictures of Peenemunde, "how the LD-27 is being delivered and how they plan to deliver the payload to its target."

"Can't really answer the first question but I would suspect the delivery vehicle is this." Forrester stepped forward and pinned another picture to the board. It showed a rocket. Bullet shaped, with a black and white chequered paintwork. "They call it Vergeltunswaffe 2."

Smithers looked puzzled. "Retaliation Weapon 2." Smithers nodded. "According to our intel, it is supposed to be what they call a guided ballistic missile, whatever the hell that is."

"Sounds very unpleasant, Sir."

"Quite."

"So, what you're suggesting, Sir, it that they put this LD-27 on the top of one of these blasted things and launch them at someone."

"Yes. Knock out the intended target and depending upon who that might be, could lessen the war if they surrender…"

"That's just not cricket, Sir!" Complained Smithers.

"War isn't a game, Captain." Reminded Forrester sternly. "We have the delivery system. All we need now; is how the hell do they get the bloody stuff there." Forrester took his pencil and traced the route from France around the coast and up to Peenemunde.

The staff car stopped outside the main entrance of the hospital, the door opened, and Lieutenant Peter Fallon stepped out. He skipped up the stairs, saluting the guards and a couple of nurses that passed him. The smell of disinfectant greeted him as he entered. Orderlies busied themselves mopping the floors and pushing patients around in wheelchairs. He went to the reception desk and asked the duty nurse on station where he could find Dianne Gerard.

"Third floor. Bay seven, Sir."

"Thank you, nurse." He took the stairs to the third floor, periodically saluting people as he circled higher and higher into the Gods. His destination reached, he searched out his target, bay seven. He found the bed and someone lying in it he hardly recognised, she was heavily bandaged, and had various tubes sticking out of her.

"Dianne." He called softly as he stood over her. His shadow causing her to wake. As her eyes focused, she recognised the young officer standing there.

"Louis." She whispered with a smile.

"No, Dianne." Fallon smiled nervously back. He paused for a moment, looking straight into her eyes. "My name isn't Louis, Dianne. It's Peter. Peter Fallon." The smile disappeared to be replaced by a look of betrayal. She turned her head away. "I am so sorry Dianne, but it was necessary."

"Necessary?" She sobbed, "I almost died to protect a man who doesn't even exist!"

"I am sorry. I had no choice. Please forgive me." Pleaded Fallon.

"Go!" Dianne screamed.

"Dianne."

"Go! Leave me alone!" A stream of tears began tumbling down her face on to her whiter than white pillow. A moment later, she turned her head to say something, but no one was there. Fallon had gone.

"How is she, doctor?" Asked Fallon as he stood around the corner speaking to a man in a white coat and a stethoscope wrapped like a snake around his neck.

"Physically, she will heal, Lieutenant, but mentally...."

"I see. Well, thank you doctor." Fallon started to walk towards the staircase.

"What is your interest in the young lady, Lieutenant? Are you a relative?"

"No, just a friend." Fallon replied reluctantly with a heavy heart. "Just a friend." With sadness etched on his face, he descended the stairs and out of her life.

18 – Extremum Fato

The waves tossed and buffeted the freighter, as if it were a cork floating on the water, as it hugged the coast on its way to Peenemunde. The bridge crew were struggling to maintain their course. Captain Mallinson cursed the day he accepted this charter. His ship, the *Extremum Fato*, had seen many an adventure over the years from the lazy back waters of the Amazon to the excitement of convoy duty at the start of the war.

Mallinson, like the rest of his crew, worked if the money were good, and this trip would set him up for the rest of his life, no matter how long or short it would be. Rudi, the helmsman, fought with the wheel to keep the ship on course. Frantic shouts came up through the communication pipes from the engine room, complaining about the strain being put on the engines and the fact that the pumps had failed for the fourth time since the start of the voyage.

Mallinson made a mental note to have them overhauled, once they reached a friendly port, with the necessary facilities. He shouted down the pipe reminding the complainers about the pot of gold at the end of this wet and soggy rainbow. Someone shouted back if they lived long enough, to get to the end of said rainbow. The Captain lit a cigarette and took a long drag before blowing the smoke out on to the window in front of him. He found the inhalation and exhalation of tobacco smoke relaxing, in a stressful situation.

The man in the white suit pacing up and down beside him, could do with a drag of his cancer stick. He took it out of his mouth and offered it to him, he declined, with a raised hand and a shake of his head, more for him then, he popped it back in his mouth. The ship veered right then left. The crew moved with the ship. They were used to it. The suited man, however, was not, and the colour of his skin led credence to that assumption. A little green about the gills would be how his chief engineer would have described his passenger, if said engineer was not below decks, complaining every five minutes about the pumps and the strain on the engines.

The passenger held up a hand, mention something about being excused and then tried to make it off the bridge. He failed, chucking his guts up in the corner. Several of the crew applauded and two even cheered. A look from the Captain quelled the frivolity and a shout went up for a mop and bucket to be brought to the bridge. The rain was now hitting the bridge windows like little watery bullets. The old wipers scraped under the attack and squealed as they tried in vain to mount a counterattack.

The Captain headed over to the map table and clicked on a small reading light which did its best to illuminate a large map sprawled out like a tablecloth. He hummed and hawed, tracing his projected course with his index finger before switching the light out. He looked at his watch, did some mental arithmetic before telling Rudi that he had the bridge, and he was retiring to his cabin for a nap, to call him if anything happened. Rudi acknowledged and picked up a pair of binoculars looping the strap around his neck.

The weather back in London was bright and sunny. Unlike Fallon's mood, which was thoroughly downcast and gloomy, since leaving the hospital. He had decided to walk to headquarters and ditched the staff car. He cut a lonely figure as he walked the streets with his head down and his hands in his pockets. A woman passed him with some kind of small dog, which jumped up at him as he approached, yapping like some uncontrollable child, the demon inside him wanted to lash out, and accidently connect with the infernal animal, but his angelic side managed to win him over. He smiled pleasantly at the little thing and assured the woman that he was not fazed by the attempted assault.

The woman yanked on the lead, pulling the creature away, before scolding it and threatening to hit Snookums, with the back of her hand on the rump. Fallon looked back at her, in his head questioning who the hell would call their pet Snookums. He shook his head, before returning to his own style of torment.

"Good afternoon, Sir." Saluted a young private who stood at the main entrance on guard duty. Fallon murmured under his breath some pleasantry as he skipped up the stairs, saluting as he passed. The Home Office had instigated new security measures regarding high priority buildings, like the one he had just entered, meaning that he now had to go across to the front desk and picked up his identification badge, signed into the daybook, and then went up to the third floor to Forrester's office.

Most of the people that worked in the place voiced their irritation at the measures privately, and a few did write memos to their superiors only to be summoned to their respective offices and given a dressing down by those same superiors.

The number on the outer door had been removed since his last visit. Again, part of the new measures. When asked, the minister responsible was quoted saying that his intention was to confuse any would be infiltrator. I suppose his heart was in the right place, not matching his head. He opened the outer door and found the desk normally occupied by Smithers empty.

"Fallon, is that you?" Smithers shouted from the inner office.

"Yes."

"Come through. Close the door behind you."

Fallon entered and closed the door just as Forrester was finishing speaking to Smithers and admiral Lusk.

"There we have it, gentlemen. The LD-27 consignment arrived at Peenemunde at seventeen fifty-seven hours today on board the freighter *Extremum Fato*. That would be…" he looked at the clock on the mantlepiece, "two hours ago."

"Do we have confirmation on the cargo for certain?" Asked Lusk.

"This picture was taken by one of our reconnaissance aircraft." He handed the officer a picture of a ship with a man in a white suit clearly standing on the top deck. "I think we can safely say, that wherever this man goes, the LD-27 isn't far behind."

"Regarding that, Sir." Butted in Smithers, opening a file, "the subject is Pieter Titus. A chemist of some renowned and standing within the scientific community. Before the war, he was researching the use of pesticides in eradicating pests without causing any lasting damage to the targeted crops."

"I think we can say, he has progressed quite considerably in that field, Captain." Said Lusk gruffly. Smithers cleared his throat letting out a vailed apology as he did so.

"So, what's the plan, Colonel?" Asked Lusk.

"An aerial attack by the RAF is out of the question due to the projected cost in civilian casualties...."

"A commando raid then."

"No. The area is too heavily fortified, and we've lost too many men already on this mission." Dismissed Forrester.

"You surely can't mean a naval assault?" Blurted out Lusk.

"No, admiral. I don't."

"Then spit it out, man! What do you mean?"

"I want to borrow that submarine chappie of yours again..."

"Harrow?"

"Yes. I'd like him to go on a little jaunt around to Peenemunde and take a pot shot at the *Extremum Fato*, if he wouldn't mind."

"I'll need to get clearance from Downing Street." Forrester nodded towards Smithers who stepped forward handing the Admiral a letter.

"Already done." Replied Forrester, a look of one upmanship on his face. Lusk opened and read the letter, before nodding his approval, there was not much else he could have done, really. "So, at 0430 tomorrow morning, HMS Spectre will set sail for Peenemunde and God help her."

"God help us all." Added Fallon.

19 – Lurking in the Depths

HMS Spectre surfaced to recharge her batteries, just off the coast of Germany. Lookouts scanned the horizon for possible enemy aircraft and surface vessels, whilst Harrow took the time to get some fresh air. A red glow came up from the bowels of the ship through the hatch. Submarines used a red light during darkness to allow the crews eyes to become accustomed to the low light levels. He picked up a pair of binoculars and looked off to the West.

He could just make out the lights coming from Peenemunde and wondered if the *Extremum Fato* was still at anchor, and whether she has been unloaded yet. He looked at the luminous face on his watch and decided they had been vulnerable enough. He ordered the vessel to dive. Crew members on the bridge scrambled down the ladders and down the hatch. Harrow was last down, pulling the hatch closed with a piece of rope, whilst another crew member secured it by turning the wheel until tight.

"Dive to periscope depth." Farrow ordered holding on as the vessel went into a shallow dive.

"Periscope depth." Came the confirmation from forward.

Farrow pressed the button on the scope's housing before putting his gloves on and spinning his cap around. He looked into the eye piece, slowly moving in a circular direction.

"All clear. Dive to two hundred. Ahead three quarter speed."

"Aye, down to two hundred and ahead three quarters."

Farrow went to the map table and looked at the intel he had been given. There was an aerial view of the target area and a side on view of the *Extremum Fato*. He started to wonder what was waiting for them when they reached the target. This, as the Americans are keen to say, was not his first rodeo but some of his crew were rookies, untested in combat. How would they fare?

He would be relying on the more experienced members of the crew to guide them through it. His first officer, Jessie MacLeod, had been with Spectre before Harrow and knew every nut and bolt. The same went for the COB, or Chief of the Boat, Alan McInroy. A burly sort of man with armfuls of tattoos. Spoke his mind, but the kind of man you wanted standing with you in a fight. These two men would be his linchpin, keeping the rest of the boat together if things went sideways.

"Coming up to the harbour now Sir." Informed MacLeod.

"All stops." Ordered Harrow.

"Answering all stop."

"Periscope depth."

Harrow looked ahead through the eyepiece. He could make out the silhouette of the *Extremum Fato*. He was not positive from this distance, but she looked as though she was riding low in the water, signifying she was still carrying cargo. He motioned for MacLeod to take a look and confirm.

"Aye, that's the beastie." He said with a broad smile.

"What do you think?" Asked Harrow.

"Three fish to make sure, Sir. That would be my recommendation."

"Widespread?"

"Aye."

"Down scope." Harrow returned to the table and looked at the picture of the freighter one more time. "If we fire a widespread, as suggested, there's a chance we will hit her here, here and here." He circled the bow, midships and the stern with a pencil.

"Aye, and if someone sneezes, then we could miss the bloody thing completely."

"What type of fish do we have on board?"

"Mark Eights."

"Okay. I want a standard attack plan. Straight in and out before they know what's hit them. Nothing fancy."

"Agreed."

"I'll let you make the necessary computations and get back to me when you're ready."

"Aye." MacLeod went to the map table, picked up a pad and pencil and started scribbling.

Harrow looked around the boat. His crew all at their stations working diligently and keeping focused. He hoped they would stay like that when the proverbial hits the fan. Some of his crew had been replacements that had boarded whilst Spectre was in dock getting repaired. As far as he was concerned, they were untested.

"Helm!"

"Sir."

"Take her to the bottom! We'll wait there until Mister MacLeod has done his sums."

"Bottom. Aye."

Again, they got that 'left their stomachs behind' feeling as the submarine sank to the bottom, into the cold embrace of the sea. Hundreds of feet above them, life continued as normal, as life could be, during the conflict. E-Boats whisked backwards and forwards like water boatmen beetles across a pond, searching for anything out of the ordinary. There lights cutting through the gloom of the early morning like lasers through butter. Machine gunners panning from left to right on the surface looking for any tell-tale signs of intrusion.

"Silent routine." Ordered Harrow which meant that the boat was tied down literally. Anything that could or would make a sound was secured. Men talked in whispers and moved only when necessary. Sound travels through water and can be picked up by surface vessels like the patrolling wasp like E-Boats. After about an hour and a half, MacLeod signalled for Harrow to come over to the map table. He firstly apologised for the delay, stating, that he had ran every scenario possible over and over again.

Checking his figures and calculations. Double and triple checked. Harrow accepted his apology. That is why he had remained his Number One when he inherited the boat because of his reputation of being cautious and not rushing head long into a situation. The two men talked it over for another ten minutes before they 'surfaced' for air. "Periscope depth."

As the submarine rose to the required depth, on shore, Titus was coming ashore. He had been invited to have a tour of the Peenemunde facility by Von Braun. As a techno-geek, Titus jumped at the chance to get up close and personal with one of the Fuhrer's wonder weapons. They had sent a car for him complete with motorcycle outriders. That only added to his already inflated ego.

It was an open topped car allowing the inhabitants to feel the air rush past them as the procession gained speed. Leaving the docks, his guide, who was sitting next to him, explained all the technical jargon that Titus lapped up like a cat would cream.

He nodded intently, his gaze focusing on his guide, only breaking momentarily as they passed what looked, to Titus anyway, as several rows of disused huts. The guide laughed at the suggestion from Titus that they would make good crew quarters if a little time were spent bringing them up to date. Titus was puzzled by his guides response until it was clarified for him.

The huts were already occupied. By the slave labour force and political prisoners, the special unit uses to build and manufacture the rockets. Showing the kind of mind set Titus had, he did not question this, instead, was relieved that men from the Reich had not had to lowered themselves to do such menial, if not very important work, for the greater good. His tour continued as they passed several empty clearings with curious square scorch marks on the ground. The guide explained that these had been previous launching sites for the rocket.

"How long before the weapons will be operational?" Asked Titus.

"Herr Von Braun estimates we will be ready within the next two years. We are still ironing out some imperfections in the design."

They came round an outcrop of trees and there it was. Standing bolt upright with its familiar checked pattern. Fourteen metres tall (forty-five feet eleven inches) with a diameter of one point six-five metres (five feet five inches) and weighing in excess of twelve and a half thousand kilograms (twenty-seven thousand six hundred pounds), the V2 rocket. The car stopped a good distance away to allow Titus to soak up the magnitude of what was in front of him.

"You said it would be two years before being operational?" Asked Titus extending his arms towards the rocket in front of them.

"Fully operational, Herr Titus. We do have several working prototypes that we test fire to check our calculations and trajectory theories."

"This is...." He paused to wipe tears of elation from his cheeks, "wonderful!"

"Admittedly, we do have a high cost in manpower, but it is negligible when it comes to the glory of the Reich!"

Added the guide dismissing the human cost and basking in the adulation of their achievement.

The Allies would later calculate it, that the V2 project resulted in the deaths of an estimated nine thousand civilian and military personnel, and a further twelve thousand forced labourers and concentration camp prisoners died as a result of their forced participation in the production of the weapons.

"What is the range?" Asked Titus, like a child asking for the instructions for his latest Christmas toy.

"Three hundred and twenty kilometres (two hundred miles)."

"The warhead?"

"One thousand kilograms (two thousand two hundred pounds) of Amatol explosive."

"Impressive. Very impressive." Purred Titus sitting back down in the car.

"Herr Von Braun is waiting for us, Herr Titus." Informed the guide tapping the driver on the shoulder.

20 – Spectre Strikes

"**P**eriscope depth, Sir."

Harrow looked through the view finder. He was close now. So, close he could smell his prey. He took a slow three hundred and sixty degree look around. He could see a couple of E-Boats in the distance but nothing in front, except the unmistakable outline of his target, and she was still riding low in the water. But for how much longer?

He fiddled with a dial with the thumb of his left hand, which was on the handle of the scope. "Distance. Mark." MacLeod noted down the figure above Harrow's head. "Angle on the bow. Mark." Again, a notation. MacLeod returned to the map table for a second before returning, handing Harrow a piece of paper confirming the attack strategy. "Final check on the target. Distance. Mark. Angle on the bow. Mark. Down scope."

Harrow looked over at his second in command who flashed a brief smile before nodding. "Open outer doors on tubes one through four." MacLeod raised a puzzled eyebrow as to the use of the extra fish. "Better safe than sorry." Answered Harrow.

"Outer doors on one through four open, Sir." Replied the weapons officer, his hand poised over the first of four buttons. "Green board, Sir."

"Acknowledging green board." Said Harrow taking a breath. "Fire one!"

The weapons officer hit the first button with the heel of his hand. "One away! Fired electrically, Sir." The boat shuddered. MacLeod started his stopwatch, tracking the running time.

"Fire two!"

"Two away! Fired electrically, Sir." The boat shuddered.

"Fire three!"

"Three away! Fired electrically, Sir." Again, the boat shuddered.

"Time?"

"Thirty seconds to impact on one, Sir." Replied MacLeod, without looking up from his watch. The crew held their breaths. Several of them looking up at the clock, tracking the seconds hand as it raced around the outside of the timepiece, like a sprinter on an athletics track. Then, thump! Thump! Thump! Harrow raised the scope to confirm. He paused, and hung his head against the scope housing, before offering MacLeod a look.

The first officer stepped up and looked through the eyepiece. He saw what a ship was once, was now an inferno of twisted metal and fire. Three direct hits and the freighter was beginning to sink. Men could be seen jumping from the deck into the water to escape. Harrow decided that enough damage had been done with the first three fish, he ordered that tube four be closed. He looked around the bridge to see his crew jubilant at their kill, but they had no time to celebrate because even below the surface, they could hear the alarms going off and the approaching whirr of the E-Boat engines.

"Crash dive!" Yelled Harrow as the helmsman obeyed, sending the boat nose first downwards just as they heard the submariners worse nightmare – the plop, plop, plop of depth charges being dropped from the rear of the nearest E-Boat. There was silence on the boat. The silence of fear and expectation rolled into a tangled knot in each of their stomachs. Then....

BOOM!

The whole boat shook as one of the charges exploded. Fittings in the command deck were rattled loose and water started to spray everywhere. Men rushed forward with rags and spanners to deal with this. Something scraped against the hull of the boat and then a moments silence before the boat rocked again. Side to side, she shook as if in the grip of an invisible giant hand who was using her as a toy rattle. Harrow found himself wishing for the relative safety of the bottom.

BOOM! BOOM!

The sound made the crew envisage a comedian up on stage reciting bad dad-like jokes and, like now, no one was laughing. The imaginary comic was dying up on the mythical stage whilst the crew of Spectre were trying their damnedest not to die in the cold raptures of the sea which currently enveloped them. More charges but this time, the submarine shook a little less. If the situation had been different, the crew might have found it funny but on this occasion, the joke was on them, and their lives were at stake. Harrow ordered some clothes and debris left over from their refit to be loaded into tube five.

"Tube ready, Sir." Confirmed the weapons officer.

"Understood. At the same time, release some of the oil from the bilge tanks." Ordered Harrow. MacLeod smiled seeing instantly what his commanding officer was trying to do. To fool the enemy above that, the submarine, their submarine, had succumbed to the depth charges and had sunk to the bottom. "Fire five!"

"Five away! Fired electrically, Sir."

The submarine lurched again, and her bow raised slightly before settling back down.

"Silent routine." Harrow whispered, placing his index finger up to his lips. Then came the sound he had been waiting on. A comforting bump as the hull of the submarine connected with the bottom.

Whilst the crew of the Spectre rode out the onslaught down below, their achievements had not gone unnoticed on land. Men and armour were hurrying everywhere. Anti-aircraft crews scrambled to their positions scanning the skies in case they were being attacked by some super-secret and silent new Allied airborne weapon. Officers bellowed orders and pointed here, there, and everywhere like a demented windup toy. A staff car carrying a furious Titus roared into the compound and screeched to a halt in front of the burning hulk that was once the Extremum *Fato*.

A cordon of soldiers prohibited him from getting too close. A man staggered forward towards him, covered in oil, and soaked to the skin. It was Captain Mallinson. He stared at Titus with a mixture of tear and hate filled eyes. His beautiful ship was no more, and it was all Titus' fault. He made a grab for Titus' throat with his outstretched hands but was restrained by two guards.

"Why, you bastard? Why?" He asked, before he crumpled to the ground.

"For the glory of the Reich." Titus whispered back, "for the glory..." But he was interrupted by the final death roll of the freighter as it exploded one more time sending everyone diving for cover, before it creaked, and bubbled, then sinking out of sight. Titus ran over to Mallinson and grabbed his arm, making the distraught man look up. "Did any of the canisters make it ashore?" Mallinson bowed his head. "Did any of them..."

"No, you heartless bastard! None of them!" Screamed the ship Captain wrenching himself free from Titus' grip, getting to his feet and staggering off into the smoke. "All my crew are dead. I am the only one left." He wailed as he disappeared from view.

Out in the bay, the E-Boats circled their last known contact with the Spectre, like hounds chasing a fox that has darted down a rabbit hole. On the bottom, Harrow and his men waited until the pinging from the vessels radar got longer. No one dared move. Some were on the verge of passing out because they had held their breaths too long. Another ping. Longer. Another. Even longer.

They had either lost contact or were moving away. Dare he risk moving and giving himself away? Harrow asked himself as he looked first at his watch and then across at MacLeod, who tilted his head sideways raising his eyebrows. His way of saying *'you're the boss.'* Harrow slowly walked across to the firing panel and pressed the button for tube five. There was a whooshing sound and, once again, the boat shuddered and lifted slightly.

On the surface, a lookout on board one of the E-Boats shouted and pointed to a mass of bubbles and flotsam floating on the surface. The Captain ordered them to approach cautiously. Once within range, a crewman stretched out with a boat hook managing to snare something yellow. He pulled it in. It was a lifejacket with something printed on it in bold lettering – HMS SPECTRE.

"They are kaput, Herr Kapitan?" Asked the crewman.

"Ja. Kaput." Agreed the Captain sounding almost disappointed that it had ended so abruptly. He ordered them to remain on station, searching for another hour, before calling it off and allowing them to return to more mundane duties. During all of this, Spectre remained on the bottom, observing silent routine. Once Harrow was certain the E-Boats had moved away sufficiently, he order the boat to move off at slow ahead.

21 – The Pale Suited Man

News of the attack and the sinking of the freighter was greeted with different reactions by those who received it. In Berlin, the Fuhrer was furious launching into one of his now famous rages. Everyone ran for cover until the storm passed. In London, it was pats on the back all round and drinks at Forrester's club, '*The Huntsman.*'

However, in a small café in Madrid, a man in a pale suit with a carnation in his buttonhole just looked at the morning paper, which broke the story of the sinking. The expression on his face was very difficult to gauge. He picked up a small white cup and sipped the warm dark liquid as he stared at the headlines, the large gold ring on his finger glinting in the sunlight.

"Round one to the Allies," he hissed. "Setenta Ocho is not that easy to eradicate, my friends. We will be back. Better. Stronger...." He got to his feet, opened his wallet, and pulled out a couple of bills, paper money, and tucked them under the saucer. "We are not finished by any means..." He picked up his straw fedora and put it on his head before walking down the street.

He turned a key in the lock of a door that used to be red in colour, but the paint had started to flake off it. It was tired and weather beaten. He went inside and climbed the stairs. The walls, like the door, had paint flaking from it. It was rundown and needed attention. The man in the suit chose to ignore the wall screaming out for attention. He had more important things to consider. He pushed the door open to his office just as the telephone on his desk started to ring.

"Yes." He said picking up the receiver.

"A telephone call for you, Sir." Replied the operator.

"Who from?"

"Berlin."

"Ah. Put it through." The man took off his hat and tossed it on a chair as he sat slowly down behind the desk. The next conversation could be interesting. The line clicked as the operator struggled to make the connection.

"I have them now, Sir. Hello caller, you can continue your call." Informed the operator.

"Danke." Responded a male voice in German.

"Skorpion?"

"Ja."

"Use the scrambler."

The suited man reached over and pressed a button below the dial on the phone. "Scrambler on."

"Wait."

"Skorpion?" Asked another male voice after a few moments of nothingness.

"Ja."

"Do you know who I am?" Asked the voice.

"Ja. You are the Fuehrer." Said the suited man. The tone in his voice showing he was less than impressed.

"I have just been informed that 'Operation Storm' has failed. Is this correct?"

"Ja."

"You will refer to me using my title!" Yelled the voice on the other end.

"May I remind you, Herr Hitler, that I do not work for you or your party of madmen...."

"How....!" Began Hitler.

"I work for a more powerful organisation that has found it necessary to use you for its required needs...."

"I could...."

"You could NOTHING, Herr Hitler!" Cut off the suited man. "You eliminate me, and there will be someone taking my place before the assassin has holstered his weapon." Warned the suited man with a wry smile on his face. "The mission has failed on this occasion, but we will rise again."

"The party thanks you for your optimism."

"Party? Oh, you mean your pitiful Socialist Party." Mocked the suited man. "I was referring to my organisation who will continue long after you have gone...."

"But the Third Reich will last for a thousand years." Crowed Hitler on the other end of the line.

"Our analysts disagree with you on that. Especially with the directive you have in place regarding the extermination of the Jews and any other race you deem inferior."

"We are the master...."

"Race? Again, my organisation disagrees. You're just a bunch of fanatics with a taste for power." The suited man said pulling no punches as he poured himself a drink with his free hand and held out the receiver at arms-length as the dictator on the other end started one of his infamous rants about racial purity and how Germany would win the war.

The suited man's arm started to get sore after ten minutes. He brought the earpiece to his ear and waited until Hitler took a breath. "Our analysts estimate that, at your present rate of expansion, you will have over reached your supply lines and your luck no later than the middle of Nineteen Forty-Four. We are already looking for alternative partners. Now, go away. You're boring me!"

Hitler was about to unleash another storm of abuse but stopped when he realised that the line was dead. The suited man took a sip from his glass and then raised it in a toast.

"Setenta Ocho!"

22 – Reporting for Duty

Jackson Blaine placed the file on top of the pile off to his left. The K-2 of files. He reached over and placed his hands either side of the pile, pushed from both sides and straightened it up otherwise, he envisioned it toppling over and scattering across the floor like a tsunami of paperwork that he did not want to spend another several hours sifting through and sorting back into their proper cases once more.

After completing this task, Blaine looked at his computer screen and the cursor blinking back at him. Something was missing regrading this particular file. He scratched his chin thoughtfully and then it struck him like a bolt from the blue – some background information. Historical fact, his speciality. He started to type once more. The pain in his hands from the last several hours seemed to disappear as if he had applied some magical ointment on them.

'At the end of the war, a race began between the United States and the USSR to retrieve as many V-2 rockets and

staff as possible. Three hundred rail carloads of V-2s and parts were captured and shipped to the United States and 126 of the principal designers, including Wernher von Braun, his brother Magnus von Braun and several others, were in American hands.

Operation Paperclip recruited German engineers, and Special Mission V-2 transported captured V-2 parts to the United States. At the close of the Second World War, over three hundred rail cars filled with V-2 engines, fuselages, propellant tanks, gyroscopes, and associated equipment were brought to the railyards at Las Cruces, New Mexico, so they could be placed on trucks and driven to the White Sands Proving Grounds, also in New Mexico.

In addition to V-2 hardware, the U.S Government delivered mechanisations equations for the V-2 guidance, navigation, and control systems, as well as for advanced development concept vehicles, to U.S defence contractors for analysis. In the 1950s, some of these documents were useful to U.S contractors in developing direction cosine matrix transformations and other navigational architecture concepts that were applied to early U.S programs such as the Atlas and Minuteman guidance systems as well as the Navy's Subs Inertial Navigation System

The whereabouts of Pieter Titus during the final weeks of the war remain a mystery even to this day. Some sources in Whitehall linked Titus to an operation the Americans carried out called 'Operation Paperclip.

A minister, who wished to remain anonymous, linked him with the head of the Office of Special Operations, Colonel John Forrester, who had been seconded to a top secret unit called 'T-Force', or 'Target' Force, commanded by Brigadier Ted Grylls, the grandfather of tv personality Bear Grylls, in the closing days of the conflict. Said Minister was going to come forward with evidence proving that Forrester was in Germany at the time of Titus' disappearance, and might have aided him in his escape.

However, the day the Minister was to come forward, he was involved in a car accident and fatally killed. To this day, there are whispers around the corridors of Whitehall that the Minister was silenced to protect a secret. One thing that is known, however, is that Titus miraculously appeared in the United States several years later as the head of a multi-million dollar chemical manufacturing empire.

Attempts by the authorities to extradite him to Europe to face war crime charges were mysteriously blocked by Agencies unknown. He would later marry and have a son, Maximillian, who would eventually rise through the ranks and take over his father's business.

As for Dianne Gerard, she would recover from her ordeal under the Gestapo and return to a free France, where she would marry a politician and eventually run for office herself. She never saw or spoke to Peter Fallon after their brief meeting in the hospital. It would later reach the offices of the OSP, that Dianne Gerard had went on to marry a French Diplomat called Pierre Hubert and they would have a son, François.

The marriage would not last however as they were rumours that the child was not Pierre's. Dianne *would never publicly say who the father was but when questioned in later life, she would open her photograph album and staring lovingly at a black and white picture showing a dark haired woman standing next to a man wearing a British Commando uniform.*

Peter Fallon continued to work for the OSP until he was injured in a parachuting accident where he damaged his leg and would be resigned to walking with a cane. He would stay at the OSP in a managerial capacity, which is polite speak for a desk job. Fallon would head the new training department of the Agency, overseeing all aspects of their introduction into the murky world of espionage. He would also marry his childhood sweetheart Victoria Aymes and have a daughter Molly, who we have already met.

The Office of Special Projects would remain in the shadows. Assisting other Agencies with operations deemed to 'dirty' for them to handle, earning the OSP the moniker 'The Dirty Tricks Squad,' something that John Forrester fought to have removed right up until his death.

Geordie Harrow and the crew of the HMS Spectre would survive the war with Harrow rising through the ranks to eventually becoming an Admiral. His mission to Peenemunde was never talked about. Some say it was a code of honour, others that he was restricted to speak about out it by other means....'

It amazed even Blaine, how much information one person could glean from a simple internet search on a particular subject. Some of the last few paragraphs he had done from memory but the bulk of it was done through due diligence, a fact that he would not admit to unless pressed by his current employer. He took his hands off the keyboard and looked at the finished document. Satisfied, he moved the cursor up to the top right of the screen and pressed the 'send' button. The computer made a whooshing sound and the file had been sent.

Jackson Blaine stretched and yawned. He looked at his watch because, for him, time seemed to have stood still because he had become so engrossed in what he had been reading and transferring. This kind of story was what he lived for. A mixture of horror, action and daring do with a hint of both romance and sadness added to the mix. He reached over and picked up a polystyrene cup of coffee and took a sip, almost spitting it back into the receptacle as it was freezing, the warmth had long since deserted it, just like Dianne Gerard had left Fallon.

Blaine actually found himself pitying Fallon in a way because of the life he had been forced to lead as an OSP operative prohibited him from allowing anyone to get close to him and vice versa. They could be used, as Gerard was by the Gestapo, to glean information out about him and also make him make hasty judgements based on matters of the heart rather than the cold hard facts lain in front of him.

He closed his laptop and stood up. His thighs aching due to the long period of non-activity. The file next to the computer dropped silently into the box from which it had come, and he replaced it back on the shelf, being mindful to place a red cross on the end to signify that he had already transferred the contents. Blaine returned to the desk, switched off the light and grabbed his jacket before making his way to the elevator. He pressed the call button and waited.

The doors pinged opened, and he walked into the box, pressing the button for the lobby. As the doors hissed closed, he reflected on what he had just read, and this energised him to return the next day to find out more about the history of the Office of Special Projects.

Just like the door closing on the elevator signified the end of the day for Blaine, it also signified the start of another historical adventure for him and the OSP. The elevator door opened onto the lobby and Blaine got out. He unclipped his identity card from his shirt and made his way across to the security desk to hand it back in. A tall man with dark hair was standing speaking to the guard as Blaine approached. The conversation ceased and both men turned to look in his direction.

"This is the man I was telling you about, K-12." Said the guard.

"Really. Pleased to meet you." The man held out a hand. The two men shook. Blaine looked across at the guard with a puzzled look on his face. You know the kind, when someone tells a joke, and you are the only one in the room that does not get the punchline whilst everyone else is rolling about on the floor in stitches.

"I believe you're the sorry soul that has the unenviable task of cataloguing my grandfather's exploits…"

Blaine nodded warily.

"Oh, forgive me," the man apologised, "I haven't introduced myself. The name's Fallon…Jacob Fallon…"

The End

Fallon will return
in

Fallon IV

SECRET AGENT MAN

Coming Soon...